Filthy Little Rich Girl III

By

Kyle Cezar

ONE

"Good morning," Sarah said walking in to Claire's office.

"Good morning, do we have an appointment?" Claire asked wondering what Sarah was doing there.

"No," Sarah said with a sigh.

Now Claire's interest was piqued, "Is everything okay Sarah?"

"Yes ma'am, I just need to speak with you for a minute." Sarah said sheepishly.

"Have a seat," Claire said trying to smile.

"Mrs. LaSalle, I know that you don't like me." Sarah began.

Claire glared at Sarah.

"And I know that it's my fault. I know that to you, Elizabeth and Ethan should be the one's getting married. And I know you think it's my fault that they're not."

"It is your fault." Claire said angrily.

"Mrs. LaSalle, it takes two."

"Oh I understand that very well, Sarah. That's why I do not pity my son. He made that choice. But you and I both know that this is not where Ethan thought he would be."

"But he is here."

"And your point?" Claire said trying her best to hold her tongue.

"My point is that I didn't force Ethan to be with me. I didn't force him to propose to me."

"No, his trust fund did that." Claire said frankly.

It was like a slap to Sarah's face. She had known all along that Ethan had an ulterior motive for proposing; she just didn't know what it was until now. She knew that no one in Ethan's circle particularly cared for her, they were all chomping at the bit; waiting for Ethan to come to his senses and choose Saint Elizabeth. Sarah wanted to cry, but instead she composed herself.

"With that being said, Ethan needs me. I love Ethan Mrs. La Salle, and he loves me."

"And…"

"And Saint Elizabeth chose the jock."

"Lizzie has nothing to do with this." Claire said raising her voice.

"Oh, she has everything to do with this. Everyone still blames me for breaking them up, newsflash that was almost 15 years ago. They weren't even a couple." Sarah declared.

"Sarah what you never understood is that it's not what you did, it's how you did it. You and Lizzie were friends, she introduced you to her friends, and you repaid her by stabbing her in the back." Claire was livid at Sarah's audacity.

"It was not intentional." Sarah pleaded.

"I know you love playing the role of the wide-eyed ingénue, but you are not innocent. Everything that you did, the minute you walked into that school, from befriending Lizzie to sleeping with my son, was intentional."

Claire was right. Sarah's mother enrolled her in Isidore Newman so that she could meet some rich kids and make connections. When she was partnered with Elizabeth on a biology project, her mother said that the Mouton's had more money than God and that Sarah should invite her over. Sarah did. Another time when Sarah's mother picked her up from the Mouton estate she wanted to know if Reid or Ethan were single. Sarah explained that Reid was a player and Ethan was kind of Elizabeth's boyfriend. "Kind of ain't is, so he's fair game." She remembered her mother saying.

While Ethan and Elizabeth were crazy about each other they were both notorious flirts; they were also young,

4

gorgeous, and rich. They knew that eventually they would end up together, but neither was relationship ready. So they had an open relationship. They could flirt, kiss, and hangout with whomever they wanted with just one rule: NO SEX. They were both virgins, although Ethan was ready to go all the way, Elizabeth was not. So they waited. Ethan had had his dick sucked and had fingered a lot of girls, but he waiting to go all the way with Elizabeth.

"Sarah…" said Claire interrupting her thoughts.

"Ma'am?"

"Was there anything else?"

"Yes, one last thing."

"What's that?"

"Tell your son that if he wants his trust fund, he'd better stop fucking Saint Elizabeth." And with that Sarah walked out of Claire's office.

"Come back here you little bitch!" Claire yelled after her.

Sarah didn't mean to say it, but she was too afraid to turn around and face Claire's wrath. She walked as fast as she could out of the building. She pretended she didn't hear security calling her name as she walked past their desk. Her heart and mind were racing. "What did I just do?" she mumbled to herself as she got into her car. Instead of driving home she drove to her mother's house, she would know what to do.

Claire was shocked. She watched as Sarah sped out of the parking lot like a bat out of hell. The little bitch finally got some balls. Claire didn't get it. If Ethan and Elizabeth were in love, why were they involved with other people? This didn't make any sense. She wanted to call Amelia, but she needed to get to get her facts straight first.

Claire picked up her phone, "Ethan Girard La Salle, Jr." she said sternly.

"Yes ma'am?" Ethan knew he was in trouble.

"Get in my office, now."

••

Ethan could tell by the look in his mother's eyes that something major had set her off.

"How long have you and Elizabeth been sleeping together?" his mother asked before he could close the door.

Ethan thought that the possibility of he and Liz reuniting would make his mother happy. But she didn't seem happy at all. She had some valid reasons. A scandal could ruin both of their reputations. If things went south, years of friendships would be in jeopardy.

Ethan wasn't about to tell his mom the truth. It was too complicated and she wouldn't understand. So he told her what he thought she could handle. The bond he and Liz shared was undeniable, but she couldn't forget his

6

betrayal. They were also too much alike, spoiled and self-centered. They've slept together a few times, fully clothed and they mostly just held each other. But they never crossed the line.

"So you're just going to give up?" Claire asked her son sadly.

"Mom, let it go. Lizzie is in love with Carter."

"I don't think that she's in love with him."

"Other than Reid, nobody knows Liz like I do. Trust me when I say, she's in love, even if she won't admit it."

Claire could hear the hurt in her son's voice. "So what are you going to do?" she asked sadly.

"I'm going to show Sarah who is boss. I do care about her mom. I'm just not in love with her."

"Son..." Claire hated the thought of her son stuck with that little bitch for the rest of his life.

"Don't worry mom. When I'm done Sarah will either have her act together or either she will be packing her shit."

"Ethan," Claire said hesitantly.

"Its okay mom, I have it under control." Ethan said as he gave his mom a hug.

■■■

Ethan sat in his office stewing, he was pissed. He sent Liz a text. 'Call me. Office.' His phone rang within seconds.

"What's up?" Elizabeth asked when he answered.

"I need to ask you some questions, and I need you to be completely honest with me," Ethan said sternly.

"Ok."

"Are you sure Liz?"

"About what?"

"Everything, E Squared, The Takeover, Carter, Us?"

Liz sighed, "I'm sure."

"You sound hesitant."

"I'm sure about the Takeover, and E Squared. I am 1000% sure about us EJ. If I break your heart, or you break mine, it would be devastating, Remember when we were kids, I barely spoke to you for a year. It was hard on everyone, our parents, Reid, Jenna…"

"I know, but I love you Liz."

"I love you too EJ, but not like that. I think for a long time we were both in love with what could've been. And that's ok. But it's time to let go of that fantasy." Elizabeth continued.

"And Carter?" asked Ethan.

"Carter scares me."

"You care more about Carter than you want to admit."
Ethan sighed.

Not Ethan too, Elizabeth thought. "What brought all of
this on?"

"Sarah."

"What did she do now?"

"She told my mom about us…"

TWO

Sarah was ecstatic. She was sure that Ethan would be done with her. She was listening to her mom tell her that the only way to salvage the relationship would be to get pregnant when received a text from Ethan, 'my dick is rock hard, meet me at my condo.' Sarah couldn't get out of her mom's house fast enough. What was normally a forty-five minute drive took her thirty minutes.

The concierge handed her a key as she entered the building, "Mr. La Salle is expecting you."

Sarah couldn't believe the mood that Ethan had set. There was a glass of champagne waiting in the foyer with a note that read, 'tonight we start over.' Sarah smiled. There was also a bag from Victoria's Secret, 'don't go any further until you put me on.' Sarah shimmied out of her dress and quickly put on the negligee. At the bottom of the bag was an empty Tiffany box. Sarah beamed; the night was getting better and better. She checked herself in the mirror, and followed the rose petals and candles. Ethan had Luther playing so she knew she was going to get it.

The minute she entered Ethan's room, her heart dropped. "Ethan!" she yelled. There Ethan was, making love to another woman. Sarah couldn't believe her eyes. The woman was on all fours, and Ethan was behind her happily plowing away. The look on his face was pure ecstasy.

"Ethan," this time Sarah's voice was barely a whisper.

"Hey babe, glad I picked the right size." He smiled at Sarah as if he wasn't balls deep in another woman's pussy.

"Ethan, what's going on?" Sarah cried. "This is…"

"Déjà vu?" Ethan asked with a smirk.

Sarah gasped.

"Have a seat, I'll be done shortly."

Sarah stood there in disbelief. She knew that a part of Ethan had always resented her. She just didn't know how much, until now.

"You remember that night Sarah?" he asked, steadily pumping away.

She numbly nodded her head.

The look on Ethan's face was pure contempt, "you knew that would be Liz and I's first time. You knew that no matter who I fooled around with, I wanted it to be Liz and me. But nooo, you wanted what Liz had."

"No, Ethan. I wanted you," Sarah cried.

"Well you've got me," he grinned.

Ethan lay down and pulled the woman on top of him, "ride my dick baby" Ethan moaned grabbing her and giving her long sloppy kisses.

11

Sarah watched in horror. Ethan's moans took her back to that night almost 15 years ago. The night that changed everything.

● ●

The La Salle's were going out of town, so the kids had hatched a plan. Ethan said that he was staying with Reid, Reid said he was staying with Marquise, Jenna said she was staying at Elizabeth's and Elizabeth said she was staying at Jenna's; in actuality they were all staying at Ethan's. Ethan was home alone, waiting on the krewe to get there. Sarah was at home when her mother discovered what was going on. She fixed Sarah up and drove her to the LaSalle estate. 'This is your chance baby girl, go get your man.' Sarah wanted to know what would happen if it didn't work. 'It'll work her mother said, all men are the same.'

Ethan was surprised to see Sarah, "what are you doing here?"

"I came to see you."

"For what?"

Sarah licked her lips, "I just want to taste it." She said using the words her mother gave her. 'Tell him you just want to suck his dick, if you do it right, you'll blow him away.' Sheree instructed Sarah to suck his dick and then when he reached his peak, sit on his dick; and to make sure that Elizabeth caught them. Either way Sheree wanted Sarah to get Ethan to cum inside of her, and then they'd say she was pregnant. It was a win win situation. Her mother had it all figured out.

Ethan hesitated, but eventually dropped his pants. Sarah knew that she had to hurry and fuck him if the plan was going to work. Liz wouldn't care that she sucked Ethan's dick, it happened all of the time. Before Ethan knew what was happening, Sarah hiked up her skirt and squatted on top of him, just like her mother instructed her.

Ethan wanted Sarah to stop, but it felt so damn good. Sarah knew how to work her hips; her mother had been preparing her for this day for a while now. Just as Ethan began to cum, in walked Elizabeth, Jenna and Reid. Elizabeth screamed so loud that Ms. Mae, Ethan's nanny heard her in her quarters.

■■■

Ethan snapped his fingers breaking Sarah's thoughts. "Suck my dick." He instructed, pushing it rudely in her face.

"What?" Sarah asked Ethan in disbelief.

"Suck my dick," Ethan repeated glaring at her.

Sarah looked at Ethan like he had two heads. He had just pulled his dick out of another bitch's pussy, and now he expected her to suck it. Had he lost his damn mind? "No, Ethan."

"No?" Ethan questioned.

13

"No." Sarah said again.

"Cool. Get out."

"Get out?" Sarah cried.

"You heard me." Ethan said walking back over to the other woman.

For the first time Sarah noticed two things. One, she looked very much like Elizabeth; and two, she was wearing a huge rock on her finger.

"What's going on Ethan?" Sarah demanded.

"Simple. This is what you wanted. You wanted my money, and the good life. I gave it to you. But that wasn't good enough. You have the nerve to threaten me, and talk shit to my mother?" He glared at Sarah. "So I decided to teach you a lesson."

"What lesson is that?" Sarah asked with tears burning her eyes.

"I do not need you Sarah. I realized something today. I really do not need my trust fund. I get up and go to La Salle every day, and I work hard. My father pays me well. On top of that, I can do what I do for La Salle anywhere. But I don't have to. I think you forget that I am an only child. So if we don't get married, I'll be just fine. It may delay my trust fund; but it will not erase it, or my inheritance. And you and I both know if I speak to my

Piran, he will convince my dad to override the stipulations."

"I see you have put a lot of thought into this."

"I have."

"So where do we stand." Asked Sarah.

"That depends on you."

"How so?"

"I do care about you Sarah,"

"Oh yeah."

"Yeah. If I am honest, I can admit that that I do have some kind of love for you. But there is resentment as well, and I don't always trust you. You orchestrated that night, you meant for Liz to find us. You've used that night to get your way with me for damn near fifteen years. You've treated Lizzie as if she hurt you, when you were the one that betrayed her. You walk around with this nasty ass attitude, like we owe you something."

"I'll fix it, I swear." Sarah pleaded.

"You sure as hell will. Today was the last fucking straw." He pointed at the woman, "this is Heather. Heather here will fuck and suck me on demand, and will happily become Mrs. La Salle, and as a bonus she looks like Liz."

Sarah rolled her eyes.

"Oh, you think I'm playing?" Ethan snarled. "Heather baby, come suck daddy's dick." Without hesitation, Heather was on her knees taking care of Ethan.

Sarah couldn't stop the tears from falling. "Please stop this Ethan; just tell me what to do to fix it."

He tossed his phone at her, "call my mother and apologize." Sarah obliged, watching Heather please her fiancé. When she was done she handed Ethan his phone back.

"Nope." He said. "Now text Liz and apologize for being a colossal bitch all of these years and ask her to be your maid of honor."

"My cousin is supposed to be my maid of honor."

"Fuck your cousin, and after you text Liz, text Jenna. She'll be a bridesmaid."

Sarah followed instructions, then handed Ethan back his phone. Silently praying that he would send Heather home.

Ethan gave her an evil grin, "she's wearing your ring babe. Are you going to let her keep it?"

Sarah shook her head no.

"Get down there and help her suck my dick."

Sarah was not prepared for that, "baby please," she begged.

"One of you will walk out of here the future Mrs. LaSalle with a ten-karat cushion cut Tiffany engagement ring. How bad do you want it?"

Sarah got his point and joined Heather on her knees.

Three hours later Ethan walked Heather to the door. He gave her a quick kiss as well as a slap on the ass. "I'll call you" he smiled.

He returned to the bedroom and lay down with Sarah, "Come here babe." He said pulling her close.

Sarah collapsed into tears, "I love you Ethan."

"I love you too," he mumbled feeling his way between her legs.

Sarah allowed herself to enjoy his touch, "make love to me," she begged.

Ethan obliged. He took his time making sure that Sarah came a couple of times before he bust his nut. Ethan wasn't wearing a condom and he refused to cum inside of Sarah, so he pulled out and brought his dick up to Sarah's mouth. Without asking he came in her mouth, "swallow, so you can get your prize."

Sarah obliged and gave Ethan a weak smile.

Ethan gave Sarah a quick kiss, "marry me," he said with a devilish grin. He removed his grandmother's ring, and replaced it with the Tiffany.

The significance of it was not lost on Sarah, but she didn't say a word. She lay quietly in Ethan's arms until she fell asleep.

■■■

At six a.m. Reid, Liz, and Jenna all received the same text. 'She gone learn today!' Accompanied by a picture of Sarah with Ethan's dick in her mouth.

THREE

Ethan was already gone when Sarah woke up; she smiled
to herself. Ethan normally never left her alone at his place.
He left a not for her on the nightstand. 'Morning, you
have a meeting with my mother at ten. Be sure to dress
nice.' Something was up, Sarah thought to herself. She
grabbed her phone and sent Ethan a quick text, 'what's
going on?'

 'What do you mean?' he replied.
 'The meeting.'
 'Oh. The wedding is two weeks away, time to
 finalize details.' Ethan explained.
 'Oh ok.'
 'Last thing.'
 'What's that?'
 'Your mother needs to be there as well.'

Sarah didn't like that last text, why did her mother need to
be there. She looked at the clock and realized that she
didn't have time to question it; she simply sent her mom a
text. 'Get dressed. Meet me at LaSalle at ten, meeting
with Claire.'

Sheree didn't like text messages so Sarah wasn't surprised
when she called. "I cannot be there in forty-five minutes, I
am not dressed, and I need to put on make-up. What the
hell is going on?"

"Ethan said we need to finalize the details for the wedding.
Just put on something simple mama, and don't worry

about your make-up." Sarah always felt that her mother wore too much make-up anyway.

●●●

Sarah was not ready for the ambush that awaited her. She knew that something was up when Meghan, Claire's assistant, showed her to the conference room. Not even five minutes later, she ushered Sheree in.

"Oh they fancy round here." Chuckled Sheree.

Sarah was too nervous to say anything.

"I'll let Mrs. La Salle know that you are here." Said Meghan.

"Something is up." Sarah told her mother when Meghan closed the door.

"Whatcha talkin bout?" Sheree asked.

Before Sarah could answer in walked Claire and Amelia, followed by two women that Sarah had never seen before. Sheree could not stand Amelia or Claire. She thought that they were evil, saditty bitches that thought their shit didn't stink, especially that fucking Amelia. For as long as Sarah could remember her mother referred to them as the Wicked Witches of the bayou.

"Why is Amelia here?" asked Sheree with disdain.

"As Ethan's Godmother she is the overseer of his trust, therefore she must be a party to any financial transactions." Claire explained.

"Financial transactions?" Sheree shrieked, "The wedding is two weeks away! Surely you aren't going to try to pay my daughter off now?"

Amelia and Claire exchanged knowing glances. "Pay her off?" Amelia laughed. "Why would we do that?"

"Look Sarah, before you and Ethan can get married, you will have to sign a prenuptial agreement." Claire informed her.

"Prenup?" asked Sheree incredulously.

"Yes mama, I've always known that." Sarah said relieved.

"Good," Claire smiled tightly, "there shouldn't be any problems then."

The lady with the glasses opened her briefcase, and handed some forms to Sarah. "Read over it, initial the bottom of each page, and sign your full legal signature on the last three documents. This is Savannah; she will answer any questions you may have." She said pointing at the younger lady.

Sarah was anxious to sign, the prenup being in place meant that the wedding was actually going to happen. Everything looked fine. She kept all gifts, including the condo that Claire and Ethan, Sr. gave her when she graduated from LSU. Everything seemed copacetic until Sarah flipped the page.

She relinquished rights to any and all La Salle business holdings and earnings, including but not limited to La Salle Energy, E Squared, and any future endeavors and patents. Everything that Ethan owned irrevocably remained his, including his trust and the estates of Ethan, Sr. and Claire. Sarah would be given a $10,000 monthly allowance, increasing to $50,000 after five years of marriage. She would receive a one million dollar bonus with the birth of each child born to the union. If they divorced, Ethan got the kids. If Sarah ended the marriage, she would receive a lump settlement of $100,000 for each year of marriage after five years. If Ethan ended the marriage, that number increased to $250,000. If she committed adultery, she got nothing. There was no clause that stipulated Ethan's fidelity. Ethan was Ethan, Sr. and Claire's sole beneficiary; the marriage would not change that. If Ethan Sr., Claire, and Ethan Jr. all perished at one time, Ethan's children would inherit the estate. If there were no children at the time, the estates would be divided equally between their church, Claire's sister Delaney Holmes, and the La Salle's Goddaughter Elizabeth Mouton.

"Elizabeth?" yelled Sheree.

"She is our Godchild." Claire reasoned.

Sarah was in disbelief, "So if Ethan dies, I'm just shit out of luck?"

"If you had kept reading you would know that your allowances will remain intact, and there is one life insurance policy that lists you as the sole beneficiary," explained Claire.

"How much?" Sheree asked.

"What?" Amelia asked, shocked at the nerve of Sheree.

"I'm not talking to you." Sheree said nastily.

"Look honey, I am trying to be civil; but you just won't allow it. Quite frankly, you are here out of courtesy. If you don't get yourself together, we will have to ask you to leave." Claire said through clenched teeth.

Sheree was pissed. Had these saditty bitches lost their everlasting minds? "Look bitch…" Sheree yelled.

Savannah and the older attorney were startled by the outburst.

"You hoes must have forgot that I hold all the fucking cards. I am sure the press would love to hear all about how your goody two shoes son defiled my thirteen year old daughter, then strung her along for fifteen years, then practically dumped her at the alter to carry on an incestuous relationship with his God sister!!!!!" Sheree spoke with pure venom. She and her daughter had been bullied long enough.

Claire was always the emotional one, she was so upset she was shaking; but Amelia remained calm. "Are you done?" Amelia asked.

"Bitch, how many times do I have to tell your stank ass that I am not talking to you!" Sheree yelled.

Amelia glared at Sheree, and then looked at Sarah, "Is this how you want things to end Sarah?"

"Bitch, don't you dare threaten my daughter!" Sheree yelled standing up.

"Sit your ass down." Amelia said in an icy whisper. "You thought you held the cards, but the tables have turned."

"Is this about yesterday?" Sarah whispered.

"It definitely is."

FOUR

All anyone ever knew was that EJ cheated on Elizabeth
with her friend Sarah. Neither EJ nor Liz would divulge
any details to their parents, so they left it alone. Until
Sheree showed up with Sarah late one Tuesday afternoon,
announcing that her daughter was pregnant. Claire
hyperventilated and Ethan, Sr. was beyond pissed. Claire
wrote Sheree a check and told her that an attorney would
contact her the following morning. That's when Sheree
dropped a bombshell; little Sarah was only thirteen, and
since EJ was sixteen, he could be charged with statutory
rape. The La Salle's were stunned. Ethan Sr. called
Mathieu and Amelia. By the time Amelia walked in the
door she had already devised a plan. Sarah and Sheree
would move into the guesthouse on the Mouton estate.
The child would be adopted by Sheree and raised as
Sarah's sister or brother. Sheree, Sarah, and the baby
would always be taken care of. Sheree accepted without
hesitation, except she needed a car. Mathieu told her that
someone from his family's Mercedes-Benz dealership
would contact her first thing in the morning. Sheree was
pleased.

Sheree was living the good life she had always wanted, but
at her daughters expense. Sarah had lost all of her friends.
Ethan wouldn't even look at her. When Sarah was four
and a half months pregnant, she went into premature labor.
She was home alone and scared. She decided to walk the
mile to the main house; but by the time Ms. Annie, the
housekeeper, answered the door, Sarah had begun

25

bleeding. She was in excruciating pain. Ms. Annie yelled for her husband Clarence and Elizabeth. Clarence rushed to Sarah, scooped her up and laid her on the sofa. Elizabeth called 911, Reid, Jenna and finally Ethan. Elizabeth held Sarah's hand and told her everything would be okay. But it wasn't. The baby did not survive, and Sarah almost lost her life as well. The kids were devastated. Ryland and Elise accompanied the kids to the hospital; the Moutons and LaSalle's were on a jet coming back from D.C., and Sheree was nowhere to be found. When she finally surfaced, she blamed everyone but herself.

The night before Sarah was released from the hospital Ethan showed up. He cried, and apologized for not being nicer to her. He felt that it was all his fault.

"No," Sarah said as she began to cry. "God is punishing me." Sarah began to tell Ethan about her mother's master plan. Ethan felt sorry for Sarah, and knew the trouble that this information could cause her, so he never told a soul. Until yesterday, he called the one person that he knew would handle it, his Godmother Amelia.

• •

Amelia threw some paperwork towards Sheree.

"What the fuck is this?"

"It's your pimp card." Amelia smiled.

"What?" asked Sheree.

"You heard me. When you tell the press about Ethan, make sure that you tell them that you pimped out your thirteen year old daughter for the good life."

"How dare you?"

"You do not want to go there with me. You planned that night, from start to finish. You are the rapist! You stole your daughter's innocence and forever altered those kids' lives!" Amelia was livid. The more she thought about it, he madder she became.

"So what do you want from me."

"Not a damn thing." Amelia smiled.

"So what is this?" Sheree asked confused.

"It was your golden egg. It's the payday you were counting on all of these years. But now that the truth has come out, you will not get it."

Sheree's mouth dropped as she read over the non-disclosure agreement. The agreement would've given her $500,000 once Ethan and Sarah said "I do." as long as she never spoke of the incident.

"So what happens now?" asked Sarah.

"You sign the prenup today, and when you wake up tomorrow you will have $250,000 in your account. We will fly to Charlotte to meet with Allanna; and in two

weeks you'll become Mrs. Ethan Girard La Salle, Jr."
Claire smiled.

"Allana?" asked Sarah confused.

"Allana Grier, she has agreed to design the dresses."

"Oh." Sarah said with a smile.

"And if she doesn't?" Sheree asked.

Savannah walked another set of papers over to Sarah.
Sarah couldn't believe her eyes. It was the exact same
prenup, except the bride's name was listed as Heather
LeBlanc. "Give me a pen." She said quickly.

"Are you sure?" asked the attorney with the glasses.

"Positive." Said Sarah taking the pen from her hands.

"Wait," exclaimed Sheree. "What do I get?"

"Exactly what you deserve." Said Claire.

"And what's that?"

"Nothing." Smiled Amelia. "The bank of LaSalle and
Mouton are closed."

Sheree looked at Sarah pleading for help. Unfortunately
for Sheree, Sarah had grown tired of her mother's
shenanigans. Without hesitation she signed. She was
finally free of her mother and one step closer to marrying

Ethan. "I'm sorry mama." She said. She knew that Sheree was angry. Then she looked at Claire and Amelia, "I'm sorry, sorry for all the years of drama, and deceit."

They didn't say anything, Amelia just handed her an envelope.

"What's this?" Sarah asked puzzled.

"Open it." Said Claire.

It was the deed to her mother's house. After Sarah lost the baby, Amelia and Claire bought a hose so that Sarah would have a nice, comfortable place to live. They had always planned to give it to Sarah eventually; and they refused to title it to Sheree. She would've mortgaged it a long time ago.

"Why are you giving her the deed to my house?" asked Sheree.

"Everything we ever did was for Sarah, not you. Its her house now, whether or not she decided to continue to allow you to live in it, is totally up to her."

"What about my $500,000?" asked Sheree.

"Leave it alone mama." Said Sarah. "Let's go." She said standing up. Now that the prenup was signed, Ethan was hers. She was not about to let Sheree mess that up.

"But..." pleaded Sheree.

"But nothing, let's go mama." Sarah said sternly. "Do you know what time we are leaving tomorrow?" She asked Claire sweetly.

"I will call you tonight with details."

Claire and Amelia held hands as Sarah and Sheree left the room. Once they were gone, they both breathed a sigh of relief.

Claire looked at the attorney with the glasses, "Do not forget, we are not giving Sheree the $500,000. Set up a transfer for $250,000 for Sarah on tomorrow; and another $250,000 the day after the wedding." Ethan's trust fund allotted a one million dollar cash payout to his bride. Claire was originally going to split that between Sarah and her crazy mother. But Amelia convinced her not to give Sheree another dime. Amelia also decided that it was best not to give the entire amount to Sarah; she wanted to cut Sheree off at the balls. Claire didn't think Amelia's plan would work, but as usual, it did.

"It looks like Sarah will be my daughter-in-law after all." Claire sighed.

"It's for the best." Amelia assured her. And it was. Ethan may love Elizabeth, but Carter adored her; and that was what Elizabeth needed. Ethan and Elizabeth were a recipe for tabloid fodder. Ethan marrying Sarah was best for everyone. Sarah would be the dutiful wife; she wanted nothing more than to spend the rest of her life with Ethan, that's what he needed. They knew where Sarah stood, regardless of what her mother did. She'd been around since she was thirteen, and although they didn't like how it happened, she was still a part of their family.

■ ■

Sheree was livid. She had worked too hard to get Sarah where she was to end up with nothing. Those wicked witches thought they had beaten her, and her dizzy ass daughter went right along with it. Sheree was a hustler, scheming had gotten her this far; she wasn't about to give up now.

FIVE

"Hello," Elizabeth answered her phone as she saw Carter's number flash across her screen.

"Hey bae." She could hear his smile through the phone.

"Hey."

"What's wrong?"

"Nothing. What's up?"

"You."

Elizabeth couldn't help but smile, "how was practice?"

"Good. Getting ready for Sunday's game."

"Cool beans. Who do you play?"

"Your boys." Carter laughed.

"Who?" asked Elizabeth.

"The Saints."

"That ain't my boys." Laughed Elizabeth. "Are y'all playing here or there?"

"New Orleans."

"That sucks." Said Elizabeth.

"Why you say that?" asked Carter.

"I'll be here all weekend, which means I won't see you two weekends in a row."

"Well if you want to go to Sunday's game, I'll fly you out."

"You don't need to fly me anywhere Carter."

"I know, but I want to." Elizabeth could hear his smile again. "And what's up with next weekend?"

"EJ's wedding; do you think you could make it?"

"Probably not, but I can see. So what's up, are you going to let me fly you to my game?"

"Is that what you say to all of the girls?"

"Not at all. Usually, I don't bring sand to the beach." Carter laughed.

"So why the exception?"

"I figured if you're breaking your rules for me, I can break a few for you."

"We'll see."

"You dressed?" Carter asked.

"Depends on what you mean."

"Want to grab a bite to eat, and catch a movie?"

"Let me see what Reid is up to first." Elizabeth replied.

"Reid has a date, Jenna is studying, and Taj and his man are at dinner."

"So you've done your homework?"

"Yep, so what's it gonna be?"

"Pick up dinner and come over."

"What about a movie."

"We'll find something to watch."

"What do you want for dinner?"

"Whatever you bring will be fine." Elizabeth said.

••

Elizabeth had been avoiding Carter for the past few days, and she was beginning to miss him. She was torn between walking away before things got too deep, and exploring the possibilities of love. She decided to see how things go tonight. Elizabeth took a quick look in the mirror, she wanted a chill night, so she didn't want to go full on Baileigh, but she still wanted to be cute. She had on a simple white fitted tee, and cutoff shorts. Let's see if he likes dressed down, chill mode Elizabeth, she thought to herself.

About ten minutes later, Carter knocked on her door.

"Hey beautiful," he said kissing her forehead and walking through the door.

"Hey yourself," she smiled, remembering why she had been avoiding him. Carter was epic; tall, dark, and handsome with pearly white teeth. His smile always mesmerized Elizabeth, and that body, pure perfection.

"I've missed you bae,"

"Oh yeah" smiled Elizabeth.

"Yeah," Carter smiled taking off his jacket.

"What did you miss?" Elizabeth teased.

"Your smile, the cute way you ball up your face when you don't like something, and those big brown eyes."

Elizabeth blushed. "So what did you grab for dinner?" she asked quickly changing the subject.

Carter didn't bother challenging Elizabeth. He'd get back to that later. "You said you didn't want anything heavy, so I just grabbed fruit."

"Cool, what kind?"

"Let's see," he said opening his bags, "pineapples, green apples, strawberries, kiwi, watermelon, and bananas. "

"I do not eat bananas or watermelon." Elizabeth said turning up her nose.

"It's cool, I'll eat them."

"If you eat those bananas, you will not be kissing me."

"Well, damn. Can I at least have the watermelon?" asked Carter.

"Go right ahead Beyoncé." Elizabeth smirked.

Carter smiled, "you're going to pay for that."

"I'm cool with that."

"Pick out a movie, and I'll get dinner ready. It won't take too long."

"What do you want to watch?"

"Doesn't matter to me, I'm good. As long as I'm spending time with you."

Elizabeth smiled, "how about I just put on some music and watch you work?"

"Works for me." Carter said with a wink.

After a few minutes of chopping, Carter piled some fruit on a plate and sat it on the bar. "Can I feed you?" he asked Elizabeth.

"What?"

"May I feed you?" Carter asked again.

"I guess," Elizabeth shrugged, obviously uncomfortable.

"Will you relax?"

"I am relaxed."

"No. You are not."

Elizabeth sighed, and gave Carter a long side eye.

"I just want to feed you…" Carter said staring at Elizabeth, as much as she had opened up to him, she was still very guarded. "How is it that you are so open with me in bed, yet I can't feed you?"

"I said you could, what are you talking about?"

"You said yes, but with obvious hesitation."

Elizabeth was just as confused as Carter; obviously he just wanted a little foreplay. "Come here, let me feed you." She said grabbing Carter's hand.

Carter pulled away, "I'm serious Elizabeth. Can you relax and trust me?"

"I can try." Elizabeth sighed.

"That's all that I can ask. You ready?"

"Yeah."

"Okay, this is what we are going to do; I'm going to feed you. As you taste each piece of fruit I want you to say the first word that comes to mind."

"Sounds fun," Elizabeth smiled. "Let's go."

"May I have a kiss first?"

SIX

The sound of Elizabeth's phone woke her from her sleep. "Hello," she said groggily.

"Good morning." Amelia said cheerily.

"Hey mama."

"We will land at one, and are headed straight to the Savoy. Allana will arrive at noon, and begin setting up."

"Yes ma'am. We will be in the Michelle O. conference room; it's already set up. I ordered a few hors d'oeuvres and champagne. I've also cleared my schedule until four." Elizabeth informed her mother.

"You've already taken care of everything."

"Yep."

"Well, I am sorry that I woke you. Do you know if Carter will come by today?"

"I'm not sure. Other than practice, I don't know what other plans he has."

"Well, if you speak with him, will you let him know that I'd like to see him today?"

Elizabeth sighed; everybody loves Carter she thought to herself. She looked up to see if he was still asleep, he was. "Yes ma'am."

"Well baby I love you, and I will see you this afternoon."

"Love you too mama."

Elizabeth hung up the phone and looked over at Carter. He seemed to be sleeping like a baby.

"Everything okay?" Carter asked sleepily.

"Yeah, mama is just trying to make sure that everything is in order for today."

"What's today?"

"Allana Grier is meeting with us for a fitting. She is designing the dresses for the wedding."

"Isn't the wedding in like two weeks?"

"Yep."

"And y'all are just having dresses made? I thought those things took months."

"Just depends. But my nanny gave her ideas a while back. So today she is basically bringing sketches and samples. Then we will go from there."

"Oh ok."

"We weren't even sure that the wedding was going to happen until a couple of days ago." Elizabeth could tell by the look on Carter's face that he was confused. "It's a long story going back to forever ago."

"Alrighty then." Laughed Carter.

"If you aren't busy today, mama said she'd like to see you." Elizabeth said quietly.

"I can try."

"What time do you have to be at the stadium today?"

"Ten and I have a personal training session today as well."

Elizabeth looked at the clock, it was six thirty. "What time do you have to leave?"

"About nine thirty. Come here…"

"I'm right here."

"We had a conversation last night about trust. So can you please just come a little closer?" Carter said pulling Elizabeth towards him. "Relax baby." Elizabeth was snuggled so close to Carter that she could hear his heart beating.

"Let's get a little rest, then I'll make you breakfast before I head to the stadium." Carter said pulling Elizabeth closer.

Elizabeth tried to slide her hand in Carter's pants; he quickly removed her hand and held it in his. And they lay there, both still fully clothed from the night before.

● ●

"So how was last night?" Taj asked Elizabeth handing her a stack of reports.

"I'm not sure."

"Did you see Carter?"

"You know the answer to that, and thanks for selling me out." Elizabeth laughed.

"I didn't sell you out. He caught me off guard."

"How did he get your number anyway?"

"He didn't. He called here, and the switchboard transferred him to my cell." Taj said.

"Oh."

"Yeah. So what happened? I thought I would get a little sip of tea this morning."

"No tea here."

"Hmmmmm"

"We didn't have sex."

"Okayyyy…"

"He fed me, and we listened to music."

"What's wrong with that" Taj asked confused.

"Nothing. But it's like he wasn't interested in sex at all."

"What time did he go home?"

"He jogged to the stadium from here a little while ago. His car is still in the parking garage."

"So he spent the night?" Taj asked astonished.

"Yep."

"And y'all didn't have sex?"

"Nope."

"Did y'all sleep in the same bed?"

"Kind of. We fell asleep on the sofa."

"Together or on separate ends?"

'Why?"

"Answer the question Liz 'Beth." Taj demanded.

"He held me all night."

Taj smiled. "Fully clothed?"

"Yeah, why?"

"No reason. Let me get back to my office, I have so much work to do before your mother and krewe get here."

"Really Taj?"

"What Liz 'Beth?"

"So you give me the 3rd degree, but won't tell me why?"

"Now Liz 'Beth, we all know that I'm nosey."

"I guess."

"Seriously Liz 'Beth I need to get to work. You know how demanding my boss is." Taj said with a sly smile.

Elizabeth rolled her eyes, "this isn't over."

"Right now it is." Taj said exiting Elizabeth's office with a smile.

As soon as he closed the door, he sent Reid and Jenna a text, 'Team Carter-1, Team Liz-0"

■■

"What's up E?" Reid said answering his phone.

"Shit."

"So it's official huh?"

"Yeah, are you still going to be my best man?"

"Of course. I just wish that you weren't getting married during the football season so that I could give you a proper send off into married life."

"I know, but at least I scheduled it for the weekend that you're playing in New Orleans."

"True. Are you coming to Charlotte today?"

"Nah. Too much work."

"I hear you."

"Someone from Ralph Lauren will be giving you a call within the next couple of days."

"For what?"

"Your tux fool."

"Oh, yeah. Cool."

"Alright bruh, holler at you later."

"Yeah man." Reid said disconnecting the call.

SEVEN

Elizabeth and Jenna sat in a corner sipping champagne as Allana Grier and her team discussed the three different looks that were created for Sarah. Jenna took notice that Sarah really did look happy, but Cruella (Sheree) looked like she had lost her best friend.

"Which one do you like?" Sarah said turning to consult with her maid of honor and bridesmaid.

"For you, I'd pick the princess design." Jenna smiled.

"Liz? Said Sarah looking over at Elizabeth.

"Which one do I like, or which one do I think you should choose?"

"Both." Sara replied.

"Let me see." Elizabeth said getting up to get a closer look at the sketches.

Design A was the princess look and it was exactly what it sounded like, full ball gowns with lots of tulle, and elbow length gloves were added for good measure. Then there was design B, the Southern Sophisticate look, long, beaded and gaudy. They would look like they were on their way to a 1980's pageant. Elizabeth's favorite was the Modern Day Belle look. The bridesmaid dresses were simple yet, elegant. They were strapless column gowns with an empire bodice and a side split that stopped at the hip. The mothers' dresses were similar to the bridesmaids' dresses, just a little more modest. Their dresses stopped just below the knee, with a cropped bolero. The bride's gown was stunning; the column silhouette was identical to the bridesmaids' gowns with a few exceptions. The empire bodice was covered in soft pink Swarovski crystals, and it also had a detachable chapel train.

"Honestly, the princess look is all you Sarah." Elizabeth smiled. "But it's your wedding day, and you only get one; so if we're going to do this I say let's show all the way out. Let's go with C, the gown is exquisite and the bridesmaids' dresses offer simple elegance."

Sarah looked hesitant, "I don't know."

"Why not?" asked Claire.

"It's your wedding baby, just cause they payin for it don't mean they get to tell you what to wear?" piped Sheree.

"Can we mix and match from the three?" asked Sarah.

"It's your wedding hun, I'm here for you." Smiled Allana.

"Which one do you like mama?" Sarah asked Sheree.

"You know I'm all about the bling!!! Like Liz said, lets show out!!!"

Amelia and Claire exchanged glances. "So you like the mother of the bride dress from B?" Claire asked. The dress was a simple short-sleeved shift; the neckline and sleeves were covered in bugle beads and crystals. The dress itself was covered in sequins.

"I shole do, that's all me right there." Sheree said grinning like a Cheshire cat. "Shiiiiid, I might catch me a rich man."

Everyone just looked at Sheree, but no one bothered to say a word.

Amelia smiled at Sarah, "what are you thinking dear?"

"I really like B as well."

Jenna took a swig of champagne. She wanted to kill EJ, "this bitch is going to have us looking like uncouth, blinged out new money." She whispered to Elizabeth. "A hot shitty mess." She added, taking another sip.

Elizabeth took another sip of champagne and giggled. She didn't know who she wanted to kill first, her mother, her nanny, or that damn EJ.

"I have an idea," Sarah said. "Mama and I will wear B, since she's the mother of the bride; we'll have the same motif going. And you guys can choose between A and C."

Jenna smiled, now this she could handle. She and Elizabeth gave each other a knowing glance, "C!" They said in unison.

The designer took notes and got out her measuring tape. As the bride, Sarah went first, then Sheree. Their dresses fit well; they just needed a few adjustments. Jenna went next. Allana oohed and ahhed over Jenna, with her long and lean, model-thin body her dress fit perfectly.

"What dresses did you guys decide on?" Elizabeth asked her mother and godmother.

"C" said Claire. "My dress will be pearl white, and your mother's a soft blush."

"That will be pretty." Elizabeth smiled. "What about Ms. Annie and Ms. Mae, they will need dresses."

"I didn't even think of that." Sarah sighed

"Who are they?" Asked Allana.

"They are Ethan and Elizabeth's nannies, they helped to raise them." Sarah said.

"Get me their measurements; I'll work on something special just for them."

"Thank you so much." Said Claire.

"Everything is coming together perfectly Sarah." Elizabeth said. She was genuinely happy for Sarah. This was her dream come true.

Sarah smiled, "as long as I get to marry Ethan I'm good. We could all wear potato sacks as far as I'm concerned." For a split second the tension left the room as everyone laughed.

"Do you know how much women pay to have an ass and tits like yours?" Allana exclaimed as she was getting Elizabeth into her dress.

Elizabeth just laughed.

Allana glanced at Sarah, "Good thing she and the groom are family. Ain't no way in hell would she be standing next to me in this dress on my wedding day!!"

"If only you knew." Jenna said taking another swig of champagne.

• •

Carter smiled at his phone; Elizabeth had sent him a picture of her in her dress.

"That's you player?" asked his teammate JD looking over his shoulder.

"Something like that." Carter smiled.

"Nigga you better lock her down, she's bad as fuck!" JD exclaimed.

"Who y'all talking 'bout?" asked Garrett

"Carter got a girl, but he actin like he ain't feeling her." JD said.

"Old girl?" Garrett smirked.

"Oh, you met her?" JD asked.

"Sorta." Garrett answered.

"Is she really that fine in person?" JD asked sounding like a lustful kid.

"Finer," Garrett said licking his lips.

Carter looked at Garrett, "Don't play yourself."

"I'm just answering the man's question." Garrett laughed.

"Don't worry about him C. But she is fine tho. Damn, now a nigga wish I'd have listened to my daddy." JD said.

"About what?"

"He always tried to get me to play quarterback, cause he said they get the best pussy."

Carter couldn't help but laugh. "Oh yeah?"

"Catch a few more touchdowns player, and bitches will start throwing pussy your way." Garrett said with a slick laugh.

"Nigga how would you know?" laughed Carter.

"How would I know?" repeated Garrett.

"You heard me."

"Why don't you ask your bitch" Garrett said nastily.

"What?" Carter said getting in Garrett's face.

"Nigga, you heard me. Ask your ..." Whap. Garrett hit the floor before he could finish.

JD jumped in between them, "Bruh, calm down. You already know that nigga Garrett is a hater."

"He needs to watch his mouth." Carter said angrily.

"He do. But damn man, we got the Saints this week. We need you on the field." JD explained to Carter.

"So it's like that C?" asked Garrett holding his jaw.

"Look man, you need to watch your mouth." Carter said extending his hand to Garrett in an attempt to help him up.

"Yeah, my nigga. Whatever." Garrett said pushing Carter's hand aside.

"I apologize. I shouldn't have punched you."

"Like I said whatever." Garrett said walking towards the showers.

"Let me get my black ass outta here." Carter huffed.

EIGHT

"Is it safe for me to come in?" Taj asked peeking his head in the door.

"Come on in." Sheree said obviously tipsy.

"Elizabeth, I have a Carter Henderson here to see you." Taj smiled.

"Is that your boo thang er'body been talkin bout?" Sheree exclaimed. "Brang his ass here."

Jenna who was a little tipsy herself started giggling uncontrollably. Claire and Amelia were obviously aggravated, and Sarah looked horrified.

"Tell him that I'll be out in a few." Elizabeth said.

"It'll be more than a few," said Allana. "I still need take photographs."

"Photographs?" Elizabeth asked.

"Yes, since we have mixed and matched the designs, as well as colors I need to make sure that you guys will flow on the big day. Although we are going with two different styles, you still need to complement one another and look like you are all a part of the same wedding party." Allana explained.

"I didn't think of that." Chimed Sarah.

"It's okay, but you will not say that you were styled by Allana Grier all the while looking a hot mess."

"Taj, just bring him in, we're all dressed." Claire said.

"Yes ma'am." Taj said. He and Carter were back within seconds.

Allana and her team stared at Carter and all of his male perfection. Amelia and Claire both sat there smiling from ear to ear.

"So nice of you to stop by Carter." Claire said quickly giving him a hug.

"Just wanted to say hello. Sorry about how I am dressed, I just left practice."

"No need to apologize, we are just pleased that you could stop by." Amelia added hugging Carter as well.

Elizabeth shook her head at her mother and godmother; they were acting like a pair of giddy schoolgirls. Although she was embarrassed by their behavior, she couldn't help but smile as Carter planted a kiss on her cheek. "Hey beautiful."

"Hey yourself." Elizabeth smiled. "How has your day been?"

"Perfect, now that I've seen you." For a moment, Elizabeth and Carter stood smiling at one another as if they were the only two people in the room.

"Ain't none of y'all gone introduce me to this fine ass lil boy?" Sheree asked breaking their moment.

"Hey Carter." Sighed Sarah.

"Hey Sarah, getting ready for the big day I see."

"Ahem." Sheree interrupted again.

"Carter this is my mother Sheree," Sarah said with a sigh.

"Hi ma'am, nice to meet you." Carter said extending his hand.

"Oh hell naw." Said Sheree. "Er'body else got to hug yo fine ass!!! I want a hug too."

Sarah just shook her head.

"Will you beautiful ladies be in town tonight?" Carter asked after Sheree released him from her grasp.

"No dear, we are headed back to New Orleans as soon as we are done here." Amelia smiled.

"What you had in mind, I might stick around." Sheree smiled. Everybody looked at her like she was crazy.

"Okay now Sheree, that's enough." Scolded Amelia "put that glass down and don't drink anything else."

"Who you talkin to?" asked Sheree.

Amelia gave Sheree a death glare, "I am talking to you."

"Look here you saditty bitch…" Sheree started.

"Mama enough!!!" Sarah yelled.

"Next time you ladies are in town, you will have to let me take you to dinner." Carter said with a smile.

"Well, Liz and I will be here." Jenna chimed.

Carter smiled, "Cool, let me take the two of you to dinner."

"Sounds good to me." Jenna said.

"Maybe tomorrow, this fitting took a little longer than expected. I have work that I need to catch up on." Elizabeth said politely.

"I won't be in town tomorrow." Carter said.

"I forgot."

"Did you decide if you were going to let me fly you to the game on Sunday?"

Elizabeth looked around the room; everybody was listening intently to their exchange. She didn't understand why Carter was putting her on the spot. "I haven't decided yet. I have to be in New Orleans next weekend for the wedding, so I am trying to coordinate a few things."

"You can always use the jet to go back and forth." Amelia offered.

Elizabeth looked over at Jenna who was getting a kick out of the exchange.

"You betta git that jet guh, er'body ain't able." Slurred Sheree.

"You guys play the Saints this weekend right?" asked Claire ignoring Sheree.

"Yes ma'am. We're leaving for New Orleans tomorrow."

"I will definitely let Mathieu know that you will be in town." Smiled Amelia.

"He knows, I am supposed to join him for a game of poker tomorrow evening." Carter said.

"Go boy. Stomping with the big dawgs!" Sheree hollered.

He was playing poker with her daddy; even Amelia seemed surprised by that nugget of information. "I didn't know that you had spoken to my daddy."

"He called on my way here," Carter explained.

"Ok. Well when I get back to my office and figure out what I have going on. I will give you a call." Elizabeth said.

"Cool." Carter said giving her a quick kiss. "You look beautiful." He then turned to Amelia and Claire "I will probably see you ladies in a couple of days. Nice seeing you again Sarah, hopefully I will see you later Jenna. And Ms. Sheree it was a pleasure to meet you." Carter said exiting the room. All the women watched him leave.

It was Allana that spoke first, "lord that man is fine."

"Ooooh chile, you ain't neva lied." Sheree hollered fanning herself. "You needta scoop that boy up Liz!!! He is fine, and the way he looks at you!!!! Oooooh, I'd kill fa a man to look at my ass that way!!!!"

▪▪▪

Elizabeth and Jenna waved goodbye to everyone as their car pulled away from the Savoy.

"So what's up?" Jenna asked.

"Bitch don't what's up me." Elizabeth said.

"Well damn. What did I do?" Jenna laughed.

"Not a damn thing. You just threw me under the bus, volunteering us to hang out tonight. Then my dad is inviting him to play poker. Like what the hell?"

"Calm down B. But it's your damn fault; you put it on that man." Jenna was still laughing.

Elizabeth glared at Jenna and rolled her eyes; "get your drunk ass in here bitch, we got work to do." Elizabeth finally laughed.

NINE

Elizabeth received a text from Jenna, 'I feel like shit, too much champagne. Give my apologies to Carter.'

'You ain't slick.' Elizabeth text back.

"Jenna isn't coming." Elizabeth rolled her eyes at Reid.

"In that case, I'm out." Reid said.

"Why?"

"So you and Carter can chill. I'm not trying to be the third wheel."

"Well, what are you going to do?" Elizabeth asked.

"You know me, I got a lil biddie stashed away." Reid laughed.

"I guess." Said Elizabeth.

"I love you Lizzie B, but I'm out." Reid said giving her a quick peck on the cheek.

"I can't believe this." Elizabeth whined.

"Get over it," smiled Reid. "Seriously, you need to stop this. Just relax and see where things go. But you definitely need to stop acting like a whiny baby. It's not a good look." Reid said before walking out of the door.

∙∙

Elizabeth sat staring out of her window. Two nights in a row Carter had visited, and nothing had happened. Last night he showed up with steaks. They grilled them, ate and fell asleep. This morning when she attempted to seduce him, he stopped her. Elizabeth was confused. On one hand Carter was saying all of the right things, but on the other hand he seemed to only be interested in hanging out with Elizabeth, nothing more.

"Earth to Lizzie," Reid said walking into her office.

"Hey Reid. What's up?" Elizabeth said.

"Same ole thing. What's up with you? You seem lost in thought." Reid replied.

"Just trying to decide if I should take Carter up on his offer for this weekend."

"I think it would be a good look."

"What's up Reid? I know you didn't stop by just to talk about Carter." Elizabeth said eying him.

"I wanted to see if you have time to go to dinner tonight. I'm heading back to Tampa tomorrow."

"Already, it seems like we've hardly spent any time together." Said Elizabeth.

"I know. It's been a lot going on." Apologized Reid.

"Where do you want to go, and what time?" Elizabeth sighed.

"I was thinking about Sullivan's."

"Yummy. What time?"

"6 ish?"

"Do you want to take my car and pick me up when you're ready?" Elizabeth asked.

"Sounds good. Thank you for letting me hold the whip. See you this evening." Reid said.

■■

"Hey Liz. You've got a package." Said Jenna, handing Elizabeth a large envelope.

"What is it?" Elizabeth asked puzzled.

"Not sure, it just arrived by courier, no return address." Jenna replied.

Elizabeth opened the envelope; inside there was a roundtrip ticket to New Orleans and a note from Carter.
> 'I know that this isn't something you need me to do. It's something that I want to do. If you have the time, I'd love to see you this weekend.' –C

Elizabeth couldn't hide her smile.

"What is it?" asked Jenna.

Elizabeth didn't say anything. She just handed the note to Jenna.

Jenna read it and smiled. "Liz, please tell me that you are going to go."

"I'm not sure yet." Elizabeth sighed.

"Why not?"

"Jenna, we have a lot of work that has to be done by next Thursday. I really just don't have the time."

"Come on Liz. Stop. You know that between Taj and I, we can get it done." Jenna reasoned.

"You and Taj, can't do all of your work, and mine too. It's too much."

"Elizabeth. Stop being so damn stubborn. For the life of me I cannot understand why you keep trying to push Carter away. Maybe you started this for business purposes, but you have clearly fallen for the guy."

"And your point is?"

"My point is, what are you going to do if he decides to walk away. He may wait around forever, but what if he doesn't? Will you really be okay with that?"

"It's a chance I'll have to take. I told you, I have too much on my plate right now."

Jenna walked over to Elizabeth's desk and dialed Taj. "Can you come here really quick?"

"Why did you call Taj?" Elizabeth asked.

"Maybe he can talk some sense into you." Jenna said, rolling her eyes as Taj walked in the door.

"What can I help you ladies with?" Taj asked.

Jenna didn't say a word, she just handed the note to Taj.

"So what's the problem?" Taj asked.

"She's not going. Too much on her plate." Jenna said sarcastically.

"That's why you have us Liz 'Beth." Taj replied.

"Like I told Jenna, I appreciate the gesture. But you guys have your own work, and deadlines to meet." Elizabeth answered.

"Let's prioritize." Offered Taj.

"You guys are forgetting that next week is a short week because of the wedding. Then Ethan is going to be on his honeymoon for two weeks. I truly do not have the time."

"Make the time. Jenna and I will handle everything, and we can put Ashton to work." Taj said.

"No, Carter will just have to understand."

"You are being unreasonable right now." Jenna said exasperated.

"Y'all know that the Savoy is my top priority." Elizabeth explained.

"We've got it covered. Let him know that you accept." Jenna begged.

"I'll make a decision first thing in the morning."

●●

"May I ask you a serious question?" Reid asked cutting into his steak.

"Of course."

"Are you really okay with being Sarah's maid of honor?" he asked.

"I mean it is a little weird. But whatever." Elizabeth half smiled. "I mean considering our history, it is kinda crazy."

"But, what about you and Ethan's history?" Reid asked.

"Oh." Elizabeth said quietly.

"All things considered, do you think you'll be able to stand there watching him declare his undying love to someone else?" Reid asked with concern.

"Nah, I made my peace with that. I realized something a couple of days ago." Elizabeth smiled.

"What's that?"

"Sheree and Sarah did Ethan and me a favor."

"How so?" quizzed Reid.

"If Ethan and I had gone all the way back then, we would have made it official. Which means we would've probably gotten married a long, long time ago."

"I agree," sighed Reid. "So how did they do you guys a favor?"

"Do you honestly believe I'd be on the verge of taking over the Savoy if I was Mrs. Ethan LaSalle, Jr.?" Elizabeth asked.

"Maybe." Reid shrugged.

"And maybe not... Honestly Reid, do you think I'd really be happy being a real housewife of New Orleans?" Elizabeth asked.

"More than likely not." Reid agreed.

"Exactly. So whether or not Sarah is the woman for Ethan remains to be seen. But it's not my issue anymore. Because what I do know, is that while he may think I am the woman for him. I know he is not the man for me. He is going to have to accept that." Elizabeth said firmly.

"I think I finally get it." Reid smiled.

"Thank you."

"So, the maid of honor thing."

"It's just Ethan flexing his nuts." Elizabeth laughed.

Reid laughed as well. "So Carter... can you admit that you really do care about him? Or are you still telling yourself that it's just business?"

"He had a courier drop off a ticket to New Orleans today." Elizabeth sighed.

"And?"

"And I need to decide whether or not I am going to go."

"Why wouldn't you go?" Reid quizzed.

"Work. And I do care about him. But..."

"But what Lizzie?"

"I don't want anything to distract me from my plans."

"Why does it have to?" Reid asked.

"Reid one of my greatest strengths, and quite possibly a greater weakness is my need to be in control. I can only control me; I can't control him. And like I said, I care about him; which means he has the ability to hurt me."

"But what if he doesn't?"

"I'm not sure I'm willing to take that risk…" Elizabeth said sitting back in her chair.

TEN

Carter was in bed reviewing Saints game tape when he received the text he had been waiting on.

'See you tomorrow. ☺'

'Cool beans.' He replied.

'Goodnight.'

'Nite babe.'

Carter sat his phone down and smiled. He had been trying to show Elizabeth that his feelings for her ran deeper than sex. He hadn't made any attempt to sleep with her in days, and he knew that she was getting frustrated. He wanted her to know he was in it for the long haul. It was still too soon to plan for forever, but he was totally okay if forever happened.

Elizabeth was different than most of the women he ran into. Women these days seemed to be all about the turn up, the come up or both. And if he ran into a woman that had their shit together, she didn't want anything to do with him. They thought all men in his position were dogs, and refused to give him the time of day. His father and brother and even her father all told him the same thing. 'If you want her to take a chance on you, you must first be willing to take a chance on her.' Mathieu thought that it showed initiative to purchase the ticket without knowing how Elizabeth would respond.

"Elizabeth doesn't need anything and she's used to having her way. So it's the little things that will make a difference." Mathieu told Carter.

Carter had to admit that the Mouton's wealth intimidated him. There was nothing on this earth that Carter could give Elizabeth that she couldn't get herself, except love.

■■■

The sound of Elizabeth's bat line ringing startled her, it hadn't rang in days. It was Pierce. "Hello." She answered softly.

"What up?" Pierce drawled.

"Not too much." Elizabeth said.

"It's been a minute since I have heard from you."

"I've been working out of town."

"I see. You've been in Charlotte living it up."

Elizabeth took a deep breath. She did not like Pierce's tone. "Yeah, sometimes you gotta have a little fun."

"So does your quarterback put it down like I do?" Pierce laughed.

'Better.' Is what Elizabeth wanted to say. "Why are you asking me that?" Is what she said instead.

"Cause I want to know baby." Pierce said, trying to sound sweet.

"But why does it matter?"

"I want to know my competition."

"Pierce, there is no competition. I told you up front. It's all about the fun, no strings attached."

"Yeah, so what's changed?" He asked.

"Nothing's changed."

"But you said you didn't want a man."

"Okay, and?" Elizabeth asked confused.

"So you're saying that the quarterback isn't your man?"

"His name is Carter, and no. He isn't." She wasn't lying. Technically speaking, he wasn't.

"Cool. So I can still get it." Elizabeth could hear the satisfaction in his voice.

"Look Pierce, one of the main reasons you have not heard from me is because you are becoming entirely too attached." Elizabeth reasoned.

"Don't fault me because you got good pussy."

Elizabeth shook her head, and looked at the phone in disbelief. "Don't you have a girl?"

"You never cared before." Pierce said.

"And I still don't."

"Then what's the problem?" Pierce asked.

"Pierce, I don't do drama or attachments. I told you that upfront."

"We'll talk more when you get back." Pierce said.

"Goodnight." Elizabeth said disconnecting the call.

She immediately sent her mom and Paul a text. 'Problem: Pierce Rougeau.'

'I'll handle it.' Paul replied within seconds.

Elizabeth knew that Pierce was the first, but probably not the last skeleton to come tumbling from her fully stacked closet.

"Damn!" She said tossing her bat line and crawling under the covers.

∎∎∎

"Alright guys. I'm going to send a couple of email, and then I am heading to the airport." Elizabeth said to Jenna, Taj and Ashton. "And Ashton thanks you so much for helping these guys out while I'm gone."

"Not a problem Lizzie pooh. There's only so much homemaking one man can do." Ashton laughed.

"I'm glad that you decided to go." Jenna said with a slight hug. "Have fun." She said walking out of the door.

"Me too." Smiled Taj. "Have a blast and we'll see you Monday."

"K. And take Ashton to HR; get him in the system as a temp." Elizabeth instructed Taj.

"No Lizzie. I don't need any money." Ashton said.

"Then don't cash the check." Elizabeth smiled turning towards her MacBook.

Just as Elizabeth was shutting everything down, Jenna buzzed her intercom. "Elizabeth."

"Yes?"

"I have a Pierce Rougeau holding for you."

"What?" Elizabeth asked, startled.
"Pierce Rougeau." Jenna repeated.

"Put him through."

"Okay."

"Hello," Elizabeth answered tensely.

"Well good morning Baileigh. Or should I call you Elizabeth?" Pierce responded snidely.

"What's up Pierce?"

"What's wrong baby? You don't sound happy to hear from me." Pierce laughed.

"What do you want Pierce?"

"Can't a man just call his billionaire boo?"

"Pierce I'm not a billionaire. And I'm definitely not your boo." Elizabeth sighed.

"I beg to differ," Pierce laughed.

"Here we go. We talked about this last night Pierce." Elizabeth said, obviously angry.

"And I told you last night that I wanted you."

"And what do you plan to do with your woman Pierce?"

"We went over this last night. What does it matter?"

"Pierce, what you are looking for, I cannot give. " Elizabeth sighed. The last time they were together she realized that he was starting to get attached. And had he not called her, she definitely had no plan to ever call him.

"How do you know what I want?" He asked.

"Look Pierce, I can't play games with you all day. I have work to do."

"How about if you fly me out to Charlotte and we spend the weekend together?" Pierce suggested.

"Really Pierce? You sound like a groupie right now. You want me to fly you out???" Elizabeth laughed.

"Don't play yourself." He retorted.

"Pierce how many times do we have to go over this? I don't hang out. I'm not flying you out. It is what it is."

"And what is it Elizabeth?" Pierce asked.

"Nothing, it never was, and it never will be."

"Well, I think it's something…"

"What do you think it is, Pierce?" Elizabeth asked.

"Let me tell you what I know. I know I like fucking you. And I know you like fucking me, so why stop?"

"Pierce look its over."

"No, Elizabeth. It's not. It's not over until I say it's over. Either you give me what I want, or I'll tell the world just how Elizabeth Mouton gets down."

"Wow."

"Don't wow me. I tried to be nice, but you want to make it hard. And I am sure you don't want your father to know that you're just a thot."

"A thot?" Elizabeth asked.

"Yes, a thot. A sophisticated thot, but still a thot." Pierce laughed.

"Okay, Pierce. I'll be home this weekend. We can talk then." Elizabeth said ending the call. She didn't want things to get any nastier. Next, she text her mother and Paul: 'I land in an hour and a half. We have got to deal with Rougeau, ASAP.'

Next, she text Carter: 'stopping by CJM first, I'll call you as soon as I am done."

ELEVEN

Paul was waiting for Elizabeth as she exited the airport. "Hey Lizzie, no luggage?"

"Hey Paul," she said giving him a hug. "No luggage, not really necessary. I'm home."

"You have a point," Paul said opening the back door of Amelia's Maybach.

"Now you know I ride in the front." Elizabeth smiled sliding into the front seat. As a little girl, she hated being stuck in the back seat because she could never see anything. So whenever it was just she and Paul, she rode in the front.

"What's the deal with Rougeau?" asked Paul pulling off from the airport.

"For me nothing. We've messed around a couple of times, but that's it. I noticed that he was getting a little clingy. So once I went to Charlotte I ceased all communication."

"When did he first threaten you?"

"Who said that he threatened me?" Asked Elizabeth.

"Just because you didn't say it doesn't mean that it didn't happen. So what does he want?" asked Paul.

"Me."

"How so?"

"I'm guessing sex on demand." Elizabeth said and began to laugh.

"I don't find any of this funny."

"Me either. But he actually asked me to fly him out. And called me a thot."

"Think maybe he'll settle for money?" Paul asked.

"I'm not sure that I want to start paying dudes off."

"Well, you obviously don't want to see him anymore."

"I don't."

"So he has to be handled."

"Where is Olivia Pope when you need her?" Elizabeth joked. "But seriously Paul, I just don't want my daddy to find out."

"Why would Mr. Mouton find out anything?" quizzed Paul.

"Pierce threatened to tell him."

"Let's engage him via text…" Paul started.

"Okay, but I told him that we'd talk once I got to town." Elizabeth explained.

"Aren't you here to see Henderson?"

"Yeah."

"Then we need to handle Rougeau before you are seen out in New Orleans with Henderson." Paul reasoned.

∎∎

"Are there any explicit pictures or tapes out there?" Amelia asked.

"Of course not mom, I'm not crazy."

"That's not what I'm saying sha'," Amelia softened. "I just don't want any surprises."

"Well, I'm sure that Pierce isn't the only one to see those blogs. But he is the first person that has contacted me." Elizabeth sighed.

"No one else has contacted you at all?"

"Mason did. But he was just laughing at the blog stories. Besides, he's in banking so I don't think he'd risk trying to blackmail me."

"You would be surprised at what people will do for money." Paul interjected.

"I thought maybe you should change your phone number, but then that would force people to find other channels to contact you." Said Amelia.

"I have a separate phone for Baileigh."

"Give it to me." Said Paul.

"Okay…" Elizabeth said confused.

"If I can get Rougeau to text his demands that will give you leverage." Paul explained.

"Alright."

"We'll handle this and anything else that comes along." Smiled Paul.

"It's going to be okay, sha'. When are you supposed to meet Carter?" asked Amelia.

"I'm heading there shortly."

"Well get going," said Amelia.

TWELVE

"How did you get in here?" Carter grinned as he walked into his suite.

"I thought I would surprise you." Elizabeth smiled giving Carter a quick kiss and taking his duffle bag.

"I'm glad you did." Carter said staring at Elizabeth. He was thinking that he made a mistake to insist that she come to the game. She was wearing a French maid outfit that was at least 2 sizes too small, six inch "fuck me" heels, and as always, she smelled like heaven.

"Are you just going to stand there? Come in and relax." Elizabeth asked with a seductive grin.

"I guess I'm in shock," Carter said removing his jacket.

"I'm sure you're hungry." Elizabeth said taking his jacket.

"That I am. It smells delicious in here. Where did you order from?" Carter asked, pulling her in for a kiss.

"I didn't order from anywhere. I cooked." Elizabeth said between kisses.

"Cooked?" Carter asked, shocked.

"Cooked," laughed Elizabeth. "Sit down and relax, I'm going to fix you a drink and then run you a bath."

"Bae, I'm a grown ass man. I don't take baths."

"Have you ever had one?"

"Well yeah. When I was a kid."

"But you've never had one of my baths. I promise, you'll love it."

"I'm not trying to go to practice in the morning smelling like a girl."

"You won't. I have some manly bath bombs just for you." Elizabeth smiled. "They'll relax you, and soothe those aching grown ass man muscles."

"Hmmm…"

"And by the time you're done, dinner will be ready."

Carter stared at Elizabeth bewildered. He always knew that there was a lot more to her than the sex-crazed tycoon that she pretended to be. Yet still, this domestic diva was a completely unexpected surprise.

"Why are you looking at me like that?" Elizabeth asked.

"Just didn't know you could cook."

"I don't cook very often, but I got skills." She teased. "I'll be right back." Elizabeth went into the kitchen to check on dinner. She made Carter a Hennessy on the rocks and then

went to start his bath. "Dinner is coming along nicely."
She smiled handing Carter his drink. "Ready for your
bath?"

"I could get used to this baby," Carter said lowering
himself in the tub.

Elizabeth just smiled.

"What's planned for after dinner?" Carter continued.

"Work."

"Work?" Carter quizzed.

"Yes, work. I managed to get a copy of the game tape that
you've been reviewing. And, I have a little work to do
myself. So I figured that we'd eat dinner, catch up on a
little work, and then relax." Elizabeth said sitting on the
side of the tub.

"Cool." Carter said closing his eyes. Elizabeth was right,
the bath was definitely relaxing. He was so glad that she
accepted his invitation. When she hadn't called, he was
sure that she had changed her mind. He still had a hard
time reading her. One day she seemed ready to explore the
possibilities of a real relationship, and then the next day,
she'd act as if she barely knew him. Colby convinced him
not to pressure her, and to just see where things went.
Carter wasn't sure that Colby was right though. He didn't
really have a lot of experience with women; he'd been in
love with Cassandra since high school.

"What's on your mind?" Elizabeth asked.

"Nothing, I'm just glad that you're here."

"I'm glad that I came." Elizabeth smiled, and she meant it.

"So what's for dinner?"

"Ribeyes, ponchatrain stuffed lobster, and grilled asparagus. Oh, and I made your favorite dessert."

"My favorite?"

"Yes, and I made it from scratch. Well, most of it anyway."

"And how do you know what my favorite dessert it?"

"I called your father, and he told me. He also told me that every time your mother made it, you'd get into trouble." She laughed.

Carter smiled, there she goes again. She had to feel something. Why else would she call his father? And then to make it from scratch.

"I'll be right back," Elizabeth said giving Carter a quick kiss on the lips. Before she knew what was happening, Carter pulled her into the tub. "What are you doing?" she laughed.

"I want you to take a bath with me."

"I have to finish cooking."

"Let it burn," Carter whispered bringing his mouth to hers.

Elizabeth tried to resist but couldn't. She had planned a complete seduction of Carter, but now he was trying to turn the tables. Carter found his way under her skirt and snapped off her thong. He used his thumb to massage her clit and inserted his middle and index fingers into her pussy.

"I love toughing you." He said between kisses.

"I love it when you touch me."

Carter smiled at Elizabeth and freed her tits. His dick was rock hard. Elizabeth could feel it bulging against her thigh. When she was with Carter like this it was so easy to get lost in the moment. His touch always sent chills through her. And whenever they were not together, regardless of what she said out loud, she couldn't wait until the next time. Elizabeth pressed her body to Carter's and reached for his dick.

"Mmmmmm…" she moaned.

"He misses you," Carter grinned.

"And I miss him."

"What about me?" Carter asked.

"Huh?" Elizabeth asked confused.

"Do you miss me?" Carter stared at her intently.

Yes, Elizabeth said to herself. "Maybe," is what she said out loud.

"I see," Carter sighed.

Elizabeth could tell that Carter was bothered by her answer. But she figured that surprising him in his suite with dinner was enough to show him. Why did she have to say the words? The look on his face made it clear that he needed to hear it, but Elizabeth just couldn't. He suddenly went limp in her hands. "What's wrong baby?" she asked, even though she already knew the answer.

"Nothing," Carter said half-heartedly.

Elizabeth gave him a quick kiss and lifted herself out of the tub, "I'm going to go check on dinner."

"Cool," Carter said without glancing in Elizabeth's direction.

Elizabeth grabbed a robe and headed for the kitchen.

∙∙∙

Elizabeth could feel Carter's soft kisses on her thighs. It felt so good that she wasn't sure if it was a dream or reality. She clenched her eyes shut, if it was a dream, she didn't want it to end. When she felt Carter's tongue slide into her pussy, she knew that it was the real thing.

She lay still as Carter worked his magic. She felt his tongue lapping at her pussy slowly. Then he slid his tongue deep into her pussy once more. Elizabeth couldn't pretend to sleep anymore as her body began to squirm. She instinctively spread her legs and arched her back. Carter gripped her tighter and pushed his tongue deeper.

"Damn baby," Elizabeth moaned as she came.

THIRTEEN

"Henderson!" Coach yelled. "Get your head in the game or you will be benched tomorrow!"

"My bad Coach," Carter said gruffly.

"What's going on Carter, this isn't you." Coach asked.

"It's personal, but don't worry coach. I got this."

"Is it the heiress?"

Carter was shocked that Coach knew.

"It's my job to know what and who my players are doing. But I do not give my opinion unless it affects the team. "

"Again, my bad."

"Look, I'm never going to tell you to forget women and love. Because they both make life worth living."

"But…" Carter interrupted.

"As wonderful as they are, they are also extremely frustrating. You have got to learn to use that frustration as fuel." Coach continued. "God put them here for us; they are the driving force behind everything that we do. But sometimes they drive us crazy." He laughed.

"It's just that every time I think we're moving forward, she takes fifty steps back." Carter sighed.

"I'm sure that's tough, but you gotta keep your head in the game. Head to the locker room son, get your head together." Coach said.

"Yes sir." Carter said.

• •

Elizabeth sat across from her grandfather watching him review the reports she had given him. She was nervous. Although her grandfather had encouraged her interest in business, there was still a huge part of him that was extremely old fashioned.

"So you want to be appointed Interim COO and eventually become CEO of the Savoy?" Nathan Mouton asked Elizabeth.

"Yes sir." Elizabeth replied.

"And are you asking from a business perspective or as a favor from your Pawpaw?"

"Paw, I've never asked for special treatment. It was my idea that I start at the bottom and work my way to the top. I have tried calling you Mr. Mouton while in the office, but..."

"But what Lizzie?"

"Well Paw, this time I'm asking as your granddaughter. Who also happens to be brilliant?" Elizabeth laughed.

"Why now? What's the rush?"

"I just feel that it's time to expand, increase our portfolio and name recognition."

"And f I say no?"

"Then I just have to work harder to change your mind." Elizabeth smiled.

"I like the way you think baby girl. I'm very interested to see how far you can take The Savoy. But I will not decide today."

"Well then when."

"I've been lulling it over since Mathieu and Ryland first told me about it. I'm not against it; I just need to think about it a little more."

"Yes sir." Elizabeth said slightly disappointed.

"Lizzie, before you go…"

"Yes?"

"What about your personal life?"

"What about it?"

"Do you see yourself settling down? Or will being a power player be enough for you?" Nathan stared at Elizabeth intently.

Elizabeth knew that her grandfather was big on family. Her grandmother still prepared Sunday dinner for the family every week. If you were in town, you were expected to be there. Holidays were not an option, if you were a Mouton through marriage or birth, you spent every holiday with Nathan and Cate Mouton.

"Paw there was a time when I would've told you that I never wanted to settle down. But I'm not so sure anymore." Elizabeth admitted to her grandfather.

"Does your new outlook have anything to do with the quarterback?"

"How do you know about Carter?" Elizabeth quizzed.

"Pawpaw knows everything baby girl. Even if I never speak of it, I still know." He said giving Elizabeth a knowing look.

Elizabeth nodded her head, wondering exactly how much her grandfather knew.

"So what's the deal with you and Carter?"

"We like each other."

"But..."

"Who said there was a but?" She laughed.

"You hesitated…"

"I'm just not sure that I'm cut out for a relationship, at times I can be emotionally detached. I've seen mom, nanny, and Aunt Elise juggle family and business, I admire them for it. But that's not me. When I imagine my future, I do not see myself as Suzie Homemaker. I see myself in a boardroom." She explained.

"That's our fault."

"How so?"

"We raised you to be whatever you wanted, but we didn't raise you to be a wife." Nathan chuckled.

"Paw, how do you raise someone to be a wife?" Elizabeth asked laughing.

"For starters you don't allow them to attend board meetings at the tender age of five. You might even buy them one of those kitchen play sets. And you definitely teach them how to cook."

"I can cook Paw," Elizabeth laughed. "Wait, I went to my first board meeting at five?" Elizabeth asked in awe.

"Five," laughed Nathan. "Poor Amelia and Elise, they put you in every pageant in the state, bought you all kinds of dolls and dresses. All you cared about were your pen & pad. You kids would be playing school on Sunday afternoons and you insisted on being the principal. And when it was your turn to pick a game, you always chose office."

"Wow. Really?" Elizabeth laughed.

"Yes indeedy. Listen Lizzie, if you care about the young man, you're going to have to be willing to let go a little."

"But why should I change who I am?"

"I didn't say change, just open up a little."

"Yes sir."

"Don't say yes sir if you aren't going to take heed."

"I'm listening."

"Most girls your age are working daily to have it all. Pushing love by the wayside to show the world that they can run with the big boys."

"True."

"Lizzie, my dear, you already have it all."

"Yes, but..."

"There are no buts. Ethan is getting married in a few days. Eventually Reid and even Jenna will settle down. Then what? You think you'll be content simply being Aunt Elizabeth?"

"What do you mean?"

"Love is a natural part of life. Everyone falls eventually."

"I guess. But Paw, I don't like the effect that Carter has on me. I used to wake up and the first thing on my mind was The Savoy. Now I wake up and think of Carter. Did he sleep well; did he get up in time for practice? Will he call? Will I see him? And only after all of that runs through my mind, do I think of The Savoy."

"There was this movie from the seventies, Mahogany. You ever saw it?"

"I vaguely remember mom & dad watching it."

"It's a pretty good movie, you should watch it someday. Anyway, in the movie Brian asks Tracy what was the point of having it all if she had no one to share it with?"

• •

"Three more days bruh! You ready?" Reid asked Ethan.

"As ready as I'll ever be."

"And are you sure that this is what you want to do?"

"It's what I have to do. Have you spoken to Lizzie?" Ethan asked.

"Yeah, earlier."

"How is she?"

"For the first time I'm unsure. She was unusually quiet.
Have you spoken to her?" Reid said concerned.

"Nah. I figured since she decided to stay in town that we'd
at least have dinner. But I haven't heard a peep from her,
and she won't answer my calls."

"Has Sarah heard from her?"

"Why would she talk to Sarah?" Ethan asked.

"Maybe because you forced Sarah to make Liz her maid of
honor."

"Oh yeah."

"E, do you think it's smart for Lizzie to be your maid of
honor? Do you really think you can say your vows to
Sarah with her standing there?"

"If anything it'll make it easier."

"How so?"

"I can always pretend that I'm saying them to Elizabeth."
He laughed.

"Wow man. Every time I think you're getting better, you
get a little worse." Reid said ending the call.

FOURTEEN

Elizabeth was rattling off a list of thing for Jenna and Taj to handle.

"Are you okay Liz 'Beth?" Taj asked.

"Yes. Why do you ask?"

"You've been very reserved the past few days." Taj said with concern in his voice.

"A lot on my mind." She sighed.

"Care to discuss it?" Jenna asked.

"Can't right now. I'm heading to lunch with Gran."

"Tell her we said hello" Taj and Jenna replied in unison.

"Will do, and I will see you guys on Friday."

"Ok, call if you need anything before." Taj said.

"I will," Elizabeth said disconnecting the call.

■■■

Elizabeth inhaled the scent of magnolias as she stepped out of her G-Wagon. As she ascended the stairs, she was immediately transported back to the days on her grandparents' estate. She and her cousins had plenty of fun there. They weren't bad, but they were definitely mischievous. She fiddled for her key, and let herself in the house. "Graaaan!!!" She yelled.

"Stop that yelling chile before you wake up the cows?" Cate Mouton said walking into the great room.

Elizabeth burst into laughter. Her grandmother had been telling them that since they were children. "Gran is that really true?"

"Is what true?"

"About waking up the cows…"

"Well I suppose so. If they are napping, and you yell loud enough for them to hear you." Cate laughed.

Elizabeth laughed again. Cate Mouton is where she got her weird sense of humor.

"How have you been sha'?"

"I'm good Gran. Yourself?"

"Gran is just blessed to be alive."

"Are you ready for the wedding?"

"I suppose so. How about you?"

"As ready as I'm going to be" Elizabeth said with a slight smile.

"You sure?"

Elizabeth loved her lunches with her grandmother. But she didn't want to have to explain again why she didn't want to be with Ethan. "Yes Gran," she sighed. "If Ethan is happy, I am happy."

"And if he's not happy?"

"Then I hope he finds happiness. As long as he understands that it's not with me."

"I see," said Cate handing Elizabeth a glass of iced tea.

"Gran, there is no need for you to serve me. I can get it myself."

"I know that, but I want to. I enjoy it."

"Do you really?" Elizabeth asked skeptically.

"Yes, I do. There is no greater joy than taking care of my family." Cate smiled.

"If you say so."

"I do Miss Sassy. Lizzie, in my day you married who you were told, settled down, and had babies until the good lord said you couldn't have anymore."

"But…" Elizabeth began to interrupt.

"Wait, sha'. Here me out."

"Yes ma'am."

"I did not always love your pawpaw. I did like him though, and I thought he was handsome. But that was about it."

"Wow." Said Elizabeth.

"And now, I can't imagine my life with anyone else. Can't imagine anyone else fathering my boys."

"I hear you Gran. But when I look at my future, I really do not see Ethan in that way."

"And that's fine."

"And just because things worked out for you and Paw does not mean they will work for me and EJ."

"Who said they have to?"

"I am so confused right now Gran."

"That's because you keep interrupting me." Cate laughed.

"I'm sorry Gran."

"Anyway, I know you get sick of all of the "only girl" stories. So this won't be one." Cate laughed. "But I will tell you this; my only wish for my only girl is that she has every single thing her heart desires."

"Thank you Gran." Elizabeth smiled.

"So. If you want to be COO, make Paw say yes. And it's okay to not love Ethan."

"Yes ma'am."

"And it's also okay if you love Carter."

Elizabeth smiled.

"Paw told me that you all had a lil chat about Carter."

"We did."

"Lizzie, loving Carter doesn't mean you have to give up your goals and aspirations. He may be the one. But maybe he's not. And if he's not, so what."

"But I don't…"

"Want to get hurt?" Cate finished her sentence. "Who does Lizzie?"

"No one I guess."

"Exactly. Lil girl, gran did not instill a spirit of fear in you, I taught you to be fearless."

"I know. Can I tell you something Gran?"

"Of course."

"I have not been completely honest with everyone."

"About?"

"Carter."

"What about him?"

"Well, when I decided I wanted to take over The Savoy, I thought that it might help if I appeared to be a little more mature." Elizabeth explained.

"And…"

"And what better way to express your maturity, than to appear to be ready to settle down." Elizabeth sighed.

"So you and Carter are faking it?" Kate asked skeptically.

"Not exactly, he has no clue."

"So you're faking it."

"Not really."

"Did you know Carter before you hatched this plan?"

"Yeah, we hung out a few times. And I do like him. A lot."

"Hmph. Poor Carter. I feel sorry for the kid."

"Am I that bad?" Elizabeth laughed.

"Not at all." Kate laughed. "But the poor kid has probably had more background checks ran on him in the past few weeks than he has in his entire life."

"Oh Gosh." Elizabeth laughed.

"Seriously though, Carter is lucky to have found you. Or I guess that you found him."

"You're only saying that because I'm your granddaughter."

"No, I'm saying it because it's true. You're fiercely loyal Lizzie. And you're used to getting your own way."

"How does that make him lucky?"

"Because he's the one. And once you decide to let your guard down, you'll realize it."

"How do you know that Carter is the one, and not EJ?"

"Ethan Junior was never the one. I'm just glad you figured it out before it was too late."

"And Carter is?"

"Yep."

"You seem so sure."

"Because I am. I've seen pictures. He has a different look when he's with you. Know what else?"

"Ma'am?"

"Ethan Junior always has been and always will be a spoiled selfish brat. Had you guys married, you'd push him to be greater, and your dreams would be by the wayside. Carter doesn't need you to be who he is. He wants to be better for you. There is a difference."

"I can see where you're coming from."

"Elizabeth, you do know your grandfather is going to appoint you CEO. It's just a matter of time, but it will happen. Do you really think Ethan would be okay with you being more successful than he is?"

"Probably not."

"Definitely not. Carter on the other hand, is enamored with your brains. He's proud of your drive."

"How do you know that Gran?"

"Gran knows these things. And he told your father, and your father told me." Cate laughed.

Elizabeth smiled.

"Cater can offer you the only thing you need that money can't buy." Cate said seriously.

"What's that Gran?"

"Love. Real, true and unconditional love."

FIFTEEN

Ethan had Heather bent over a recliner fucking her mercilessly.

"I love the way you fuck me baby." Heather moaned.

"Yeah?" Ethan asked increasing his pace.

"Oh my god yes!!! Don't stop!" She screamed as she came.

Ethan pulled out and stuck his dick in her mouth. He looked down at Heather and frowned. When he first started fucking her he would pretend that she was Elizabeth. But ever since he had actually fucked Liz, it just wasn't the same. He had been trying to figure out how to get Elizabeth back, but he kept drawing a blank. Until Heather called him a couple of hours ago. She wanted to give him a taste of what he'd be missing once he married Sarah. That's when Ethan devised his plan. It wasn't the right or nicest thing to do. But it was time he got what he wanted. He was tired of being nice; nice is what had landed him where he was.

∎∎∎

Elizabeth knocked on Carter's door. After speaking with her grandmother she felt the urge to see him. So she hopped a plane to Charlotte. Now she was standing at his door.

"Hey bae," Carter said opening his door.

Elizabeth could tell that he was shocked. "Is it okay if I come in?" She asked.

"Of course," he said pulling her inside.

"You know what happened last time we had a falling out," she laughed.

"That was then," Carter said giving Elizabeth a hug.

"I've missed you," Elizabeth whispered.

Carter smiled and held her tighter. "I've missed you too," he said giving her a gentle kiss on the top of her head.

"What were you doing?"

"Reviewing game tape."

"I'm sorry. I didn't mean to interrupt."

"It's okay. You mind watching it with me?"

"Not at all." Elizabeth smiled.

"Let's go," Carter said heading towards his media room.

"Wait, I need to tell you something."

"I don't like the sound of this," Carter sighed.

"It's not bad."

"Well shoot," he said still unsure.

"Carter, look." Elizabeth sighed. "I'm tired of running from whatever is happening between us. I care about you, a lot."

"You do?" He smiled.

"I do. Please don't make me regret it."

"I promise that I won't," Carter smiled. It wasn't the declaration of love that he'd hoped for. But he was satisfied, because he knew that it was from her heart.

● ●

Taj burst into Jenna's office obviously upset. "Oh my God Jenna, Liz 'Beth is going to be livid."

"What's wrong?" Jenna asked puzzled.

"This!!" Taj said pushing his iPad in Jenna's face.

"Oh hell no!" Jenna said not believing her eyes.

"Same thing Ashton said when he called me."

"I cannot believe Carter would fuck up like this!!! I was rooting for him!" Jenna said, agitated.

"I'm trying to get it taken down before Mizz Amelia sees it," Taj sighed.

"Carter had better pray that she doesn't see it. And Lord, if Mathieu sees it, he will be lucky to play another inning."

"Football has quarters," Taj laughed.

"Those too. I just can't believe that bastard would cheat on B like that." Jenna fumed.

"Wait, what?" asked Taj confused.

Jenna looked at Taj not understanding why he was confused. Just then her cell rang, it was Ethan. "What's up EJ?" she answered.

"Yooooo, did you see The Blog?" he said laughing.

"Looking at it now. It's not funny."

"Can you believe this dude?" Ethan asked.

"Hell no. And it's a good thing B kept her guard up." Jenna sighed.

"I know. But I told y'all that he wasn't shit. But noooo, y'all didn't wanna listen. All in the lobby talking about he loves Liz, then he pulls some shit like this."

"Wait, that's not Liz 'Beth?" Taj asked.

"Hell no. She's a knockoff... A good one though I must admit." Jenna replied.

"Then to do that shit in New Orleans, with Liz there. That must be why she didn't go back to Charlotte." Ethan said.

"Say what now?" Jenna said alarmed.

"Oh, so y'all saw the picture but didn't read the whole story?" Ethan asked.

"We'll call you back." Jenna said disconnecting the call.

"So that's not Liz 'Beth?" Taj asked again sinking into a chair. This was far worse than he originally thought.

"No, it's not."

"But she looks just like her." Taj sighed.

"Until you look closely. B has a mole, this chick doesn't. Knockoff has a tattoo, B doesn't."

"Wow." Said Taj. "Who is she? And do you think maybe she fooled Carter?"

"That's what we need to find out."

● ●

"Damn, what the hell is going on?" Carter said noticing that he had over one hundred missed calls, as he and Elizabeth returned from a morning jog.

"Whatever it is, it can't be good." Elizabeth replied noticing she had several missed calls as well.

"What the fuck!" they both exclaimed in unison.

Elizabeth stared at a picture that Ethan sent her. It was Carter and a woman that looked eerily similar to her. He had her bent over a chair, with his head buried in her hair. There was another picture included that showed her exiting Carter's hotel room in New Orleans. According to Ethan, the blogs thought the woman was actually Elizabeth.

Carter was staring at the same set of pictures, only his were sent by Garrett. Garrett believed the female to be Elizabeth. According to Garrett the blog that posted the pictures also insinuated that there might also be a sex tape.

"Elizabeth," Carter began.

"What?"

"Listen…"

"So did you fuck her before I got to New Orleans or after our little fight?"

"Elizabeth, I spent my first night in New Orleans playing poker with your dad and his buddies."

"So after then?"

"No bae, it didn't happen at all!!!"

"Carter. Seriously. You're going to stand there and lie to my face when I'm staring at a picture of you balls deep in some pussy?"

"Just like the female is not you, the guy is not I!!!"

"Carter, there are pictures of her leaving your hotel room."

"It's a hotel bae. Not my house. You really think that's me?"

"I knew this shit would happen."

"You knew what would happen?" Carter asked angrily.

"This, right here. This bullshit." Elizabeth said, throwing the phone at Carter.

"Come on bae. Please don't do this?"

"I'm not doing anything."

"Elizabeth. The night you called me to set up the little threesome, I had a date. But I canceled it."

"What does that have to do with anything?"

"Everything."

"How so?"

"Bae, listen to me. I haven't slept with anyone but you since that night."

"What about the day I caught you and the little skank together?"

"Why bring that back up?"

"Because its evidence of a pattern Carter. I piss you off and you go looking for random pussy!!!" Elizabeth spat.

"Wow."

"Wow, what?"

"Bae, please tell me what to do?"

"How about not fuck heauxs! Simple."

"You know damn well that's not me."

"I don't know a damn thing."

....

Reid looked at the article on The Blog and shook his head. He tried his best to never visit that site because they tended not to fact check. As soon as he saw the picture he knew the female was not Elizabeth, and he hoped like hell that the faceless dude was not Carter.

SIXTEEN

"Really Ethan!!!" Sarah exclaimed walking into his office.

"What now, Sarah?" he asked, annoyed.

"You know what."

"I really don't. But you need to make it quick; I have work to do before this damn wedding."

"Why did you do this Ethan?" Sarah asked.

"Do what?"

"Never mind." Sarah said turning around and walking out of the door.

Sarah was excited to hear that The Blog had nude pictures of Elizabeth. The thought of Saint Elizabeth being dethroned made her warm and fuzzy inside, she laughed to herself, until she saw the pictures. Sarah knew Heather's trashy hummingbird tattoo anywhere. And although his face wasn't visible, she knew the man in the photos was Ethan. What Sarah could not figure out was why Ethan would embarrass Elizabeth in this way. Or why he would create such havoc days before the wedding.

∙∙∙

Colby stared at the pictures. The one thing on their side was that Carter had never been involved in a scandal of any kind. He just wanted to know where the pictures came from, and if Carter and Elizabeth were intentionally misidentified. Carter sounded so distraught when he called Colby. He wanted the source of the picture identified and prosecuted.

It was now clear that the female in the picture was not Elizabeth, so she was in the clear and Carter was being blasted as a cheater. The Panthers front office was scrambling to help clear Carter's name. He had a squeaky-clean boy next-door image, and they wanted to keep it that way.

"Kayla, can you come in here for a minute?" Colby said buzzing his assistant.

"Coming…"

"What have you found out?" he asked as Kayla walked into his office.

"Nothing yet, but I do have an idea."

"What's that?"

"Maybe we should send a baller mail to Baller Alert?"

"A what?"

"Baller mail. It's a feature on Baller Alerts site."

"Okay and what is Baller Alert, and how will this help Carter?" Colby asked skeptically.

"Baller Alert is a website for those that want the ballerific life. People wrongly assume it's a site for groupies, but there's so much more to it than that." Kayla explained.

"Okay, so what's a baller mail?"

"Basically baller mail is tea."

"Tea?" asked Colby. "I'm lost."

"Tea, as in news, information. We send them our version of events. And they post it."

"But gossip blogs are how we got in this mess."

"True. But Baller Alert is reputable. They were the first blog to tell a factual story about Carter and Elizabeth. When all the other blogs were still saying that Elizabeth was dating Carter and her cousin, it was Baller Alert that did the research and printed the facts."

"Ok. So what would this baller mail say?"

"For starters, Carter isn't even known as a player. Second do we really believe he's going to go all the way to his girlfriend's hometown to cheat on her with a cheap knockoff?" Kayla started.

"What else?"

"I don't know. But I'll figure it out. Tell Carter I got this."

"Well go get it. Good job." Carter said as Kayla left his office.

••

Mathieu walked into Amelia's office fuming. Amelia knew exactly what was wrong with her husband, but she didn't know how he found out. Mathieu didn't do gossip blogs.

"When the hell were you going to tell me about this?" he asked Amelia showing her his iPad.

"I'm trying to get to the bottom of it as we speak."

"Where did this doppelganger come from?" he fumed.

"I do not know Mat." Amelia sighed. "The girl was familiar to her, but she couldn't for the life of her recall why."

"And Carter? What does he have to say for himself?"

"I haven't spoken to him, or Elizabeth."

"I let that boy into my house, he met my friends, but more importantly I trusted him with my daughter!" Mathieu bellowed.

"I know. This isn't making sense to me."

"I should hope not!"

"Honey, I do not think that it's him."

"Let's find out. Get his ass on the phone. Now." Mathieu demanded.

● ●

Claire shook her head in disgust. What had Ethan done and why? Claire had no clue how to fix Ethan's mess this time. Normally, she called Amelia; but this time Ethan had gone too far. If Mathieu and Amelia found out the truth, the damage would be irreparable. And Ethan Senior would never give Ethan the reigns of La Salle Energy. He couldn't have possibly thought this through.

"Why son?" Claire asked as tears began to scroll down her face.

SEVENTEEN

Carter looked at his phone and sighed. He wanted to call Mathieu before he saw anything, but his phone had been ringing nonstop. It was too late, Mathieu was calling him.

"Hello," he answered.

"Hi Carter," it was Amelia.

"Hi Mrs. Mouton," he said sheepishly.

"How are you son?" she asked sounding concerned.

"This is bullshit!" Mathieu interrupted. "Enough with the pleasantries. I need an explanation, now!"

Carter had to look at the display to be sure he was talking to Mathieu and not his father, Caleb. "I apologize to the both of you for any trouble this has caused you personally or professionally. I honestly do not have an explanation."

"Did you for one second think about Lizzie?" Mathieu demanded.

"I think about her all of the time. Sir, I would never ever hurt Elizabeth. I know this looks extremely bad, but please believe me when I say the man in the picture is not me."

"Carter, don't you dare play games with me." Mathieu yelled.

"I'm not sir. I really do not know who, or why. But I think these pictures were sent to the tabloid with full knowledge that the people in the photos aren't Elizabeth or myself."

"Initially, I wanted to strangle you, but I hear the sincerity in your voice."

"Mr. Mouton…" Carter sighed.

"Yes, Carter?"

"Please know that I would never put Elizabeth in a position that would jeopardize her personal or professional integrity."

"I do appreciate that son," Mathieu's tone softened.

"She's fighting me every step of the way, but I truly care about your daughter."

"I'm trusting you on this Carter. Do not make me regret it."

"I won't. Have you spoken to Elizabeth?" Carter asked.

"No, she's not answering her phone. My next call is to Reid. Maybe he has heard from her." Mathieu explained.

"Will you let me know that she's okay?"

"I will." Mathieu said.

"We will get to the bottom of this Carter. Don't worry." Amelia added before the call disconnected.

●●

Elizabeth sat on her balcony in silence. For the first time in forever she didn't know which way to go. A huge part of her didn't believe that Carter could hurt her in this way. But she was still unsure. Maybe it was karma for the way she'd lived her life. She never cared if a man was attached before, she actually preferred it. A man's girlfriend or wife was never an issue for her. Now that the show was on the other foot, it didn't feel so good.

She had constantly told herself that she did not believe in monogamy; that there was no such thing as "the one." She had sat through numerous bridal showers listening to the blushing bride, gush about the perfect man she was about to marry. She'd seen her friends throw away their dreams all for the sake of love. There was nothing Elizabeth hated more than to see a woman become a shell of her former self the minute she fell in love. She promised herself that would never happen to her. One of the things that drew her to Carter was the feeling that she could be herself completely with him. Now it seemed he was no different from anyone else.

Her phone rang for the millionth time today. She had ignored every phone call she received today; her parents, Carter, even Reid. Ethan had also been texting his undying love non-stop. Elizabeth would be glad when he and Sarah were safely married.

"Lizzie, call your mama and tell her you're here, please. She's worried sick." Cate Mouton said interrupting Elizabeth's thoughts.

"Will you call her Gran, or have Paw do it. Please? I really don't want to talk to anyone." Elizabeth pleaded.

"I'll do it today, but you will talk to your parents tomorrow." Cate scolded her.

"Yes ma'am."

"I'm about to turn in, do you need anything?"

"Is it okay if I have some wine?" Elizabeth asked sheepishly, she usually didn't drink in her grandparents' presence.

"I'll have some brought up." Cate said closing the door behind her.

Kate didn't ask any questions when Elizabeth showed up this afternoon in tears. She simply fixed her granddaughter some warm tea, and tucked her into her bed.

"Come in," Elizabeth said when she heard a knock on her door. "Oh hey, paw. You didn't have to bring the wine; I could've gone down to get it."

"I know, but I wanted to make sure you were okay Lizzie girl." He smiled softly.

"I'm okay, thank you for asking."

"I love you Lizzie, try to get some rest."

"Yes sir," Elizabeth said watching her grandfather close the door. Elizabeth sipped her wine and closed her eyes. She had to admit that she really did want a love of her own, but not one that would destroy her in the process.

18

Two days had passed and nothing had changed. Carter hadn't spoken to Elizabeth, and The Blog refused to print a retraction. Kayla's baller mail to Baller Alert had helped to discredit The Blog but there were still the naysayers. The Panthers had confirmed that Carter was not in New Orleans when the pictures were taken, but the hotel refused to confirm whether or not Carter had checked out of the room. "Something has got to give," Carter mumbled while picking up his phone.

"What's up LB," Colby said answering his phone.

"Quick question."

"What's that?"

"How bad would it be to place me on injured reserve so that I can go to New Orleans this weekend?"

"Are you insane Carter?" Colby asked in disbelief.

"I really don't know what else to do," Carter sighed.

"Look, I know that you are crazy about Elizabeth. But you can't just go on injured reserve."

"Do you have a better idea?"

"No. You do realize that if Elizabeth knew you were considering skipping the game, she'd be livid."

"Honestly bruh, I don't think she cares," said Carter sadly.

"Then why do you?" Colby asked somberly.

"I just want to give it one last shot," Carter explained.

"What time is the wedding Sunday?"

"It's Saturday, at six."

"Then why do you want to miss the game?"

"I don't know," Carter sounded lost.

Colby didn't like the way his little brother sounded. "I'll see you tomorrow Carter?"

"You're coming to Charlotte?"

"Don't I go to every game?"

"Yes, but…"

"It sounds like you need me LB. We'll put our heads together tomorrow."

"Thank you Colby,"

"No problem."

Sarah checked her bags one last time. Tomorrow she would become Mrs. Ethan Girard La Salle, Junior. They were leaving for their honeymoon immediately after the reception, and she wanted to make sure that she had everything.

"We done made it baby girl," Sheree said sashaying into Sarah's bedroom and giving her a hug.

"We're not in the clear yet," Sarah sighed. "I'm not celebrating until we are pronounced man and wife."

"You aiight?" Sheree asked.

"Yeah, I'm good. You just never know with Ethan these days."

"Girl, hush that fuss. In less than twenty-four hours all of our hard work will pay off." Sheree said licking her lips. "And I been thankin, I needta move inta this here 'partment. I wanna rent my house out so I can make a lil change of my own."

"We'll talk about it when I get back from Venice."

"Aiight." Sheree said knowing full well that she had already made plans, by the time Saran and Ethan returned she'd have everything settled. "You got er'thang?"

"I hope so." Sarah said still wondering if her wedding would happen at all.

"Whatever you leave behind, you can buy later, Mrs. LaSalle."

"I guess you're right," Sarah said trying to cheer up.

"Aiight lets go. We don't want to keep Ethan and his saditty ass mammy waiting too long." Sheree cackled.

"We have to make one stop first."

NINETEEN

"Hey EJ," Elizabeth said giving him a quick hug as she entered the chapel.

"Hey, Liz." He smiled nervously.

"You good? I thought you'd be jumping for joy right about now."

"Really?"

"Yeah, in less than twenty-four hours you'll be a millionaire in your own right." Elizabeth said.

"Yeah, but at what cost?" Ethan sighed.

"Sorry."

"Have you seen my mom or Reid?" Ethan asked.

"Nanny is in the house with mama and Gran. I am not sure where Reid is."

"What about Jenna?" Ethan asked.

"I haven't heard from the heifer since she landed, but you know she'll be here."

"Okay." Ethan said trying to smile.

"Calm down EJ. Everything will be just fine," Elizabeth tried to assure him.

Ethan gave Elizabeth a half-hearted smile. He was trying his best not to let his nerves get the best of him. On one hand he was pissed that his plan hadn't seemed to work; he was so sure that Elizabeth would hate Carter, and come running to him. But on the other hand he was worried about the consequences of his actions. He suspected that his mom and Sarah knew the truth. They had been acting very strange since the story hit the press. But he wasn't really worried about those two; they'd protect him to no end. It was the wrath of his father and Godparents that put the fear of God in him. Ethan Senior would not care that he was desperate; he would have no problem disowning his only son. And for the first time in his life, Ethan wouldn't be able to turn to Mathieu and Amelia. Then there was the krewe; he would lose all of them. It seemed like a foolproof plan when he first thought of it.

"Taj, have you heard from Jenna?" Ethan heard Elizabeth asking Taj as he and Ashton entered the chapel.

"Not since we landed." Taj said giving Elizabeth a hug. "Everything okay?"

"Yeah, I just wonder where that tramp is. I haven't heard from her at all today." Elizabeth laughed.

"She's probably with her boo," Ashton explained.

"What boo?" Elizabeth, Taj and Ethan asked in unison.

"Haaaayyyy, Miss Amelia" Ashton squealed as Amelia walked into the chapel, ignoring the trios question.

"He knows something," Elizabeth said.

"Yep. Don't worry Liz 'Beth I'll find out what it is." Taj said.

"Make sure to keep me in the loop." Ethan chimed in.

"Where are your bride and groomsmen?" Claire asked giving Ethan a slight hug.

"Your guess is as good as mine."

"Reid is on his way," Amelia said kissing Ethan on the cheek.

"Thanks Nanny," he smiled.

Just then Reid walked in, "Have no fear, the best man is here!"

"At least someone is excited," Ethan mumbled. "Have you heard from Marquise or Jenna?"

"They are both on the way." Reid smiled.

"Hey y'all, sorry I'm late. Had some business to handle." Jenna said as if on cue.

"What business bitch?" Elizabeth laughed giving her best friend a hug.

"Girl. We are in church!" Jenna laughed.

"My bad. But seriously, where you been?"

"We'll talk." Jenna said walking over to give Amelia and Claire hugs.

"Do you know where Jenna's been?" Elizabeth asked Reid.

"Nah," he shrugged.

Before Elizabeth could press further Reid went to greet Marquise Landry, Ethan's groomsman, and his wife Lola. Elizabeth's mouth dropped when Lola walked in, she looked at least twelve months pregnant.

"Quise," Reid said giving him a quick dap before hugging Lola. "So good to see you guys."

"Hey Reid, hey Liz," Lola said hugging Reid, and then wobbling over to Elizabeth.

"Hey Lo. Girl. When are you due?" Elizabeth asked.

"Chile, I still have two months to go." Lola sighed.

"Dang. No offense, but you look ready to pop."

"I'm definitely ready, but my little munchkin isn't." Lola laughed. "Seriously, how are you holding up Liz?"

"I'm okay."

"Are you sure?"

"Yes. I am truly happy for Ethan and Sarah."

"I wasn't referring to that." Lola said with concern.

"Oh," Elizabeth sighed. "You do know that wasn't me, right?"

"Of course. But still, pictures of your man with a knockoff had to hurt."

"Yeah…"

"Is he still insisting that it's not him?"

"I haven't really talked to him."

"Maybe you should hear him out Liz. He seems to be a good guy, in spite of this situation. And I've never seen you happier."

"Nah, Lo. I'm good. I'll leave the marriage and babies to y'all." Elizabeth assured her.

"If you say so," Lola smiled giving Elizabeth another hug before taking a seat.

"EJ, have you heard from Sarah? Ethan Senior asked as he and Mathieu entered the chapel.

"No sir. I've called her & Sheree several times. Neither of them have answered my calls."

TWENTY

"Why are you doing this?" Carter asked Sarah.

"Because Elizabeth has suffered enough because of me. And because it's the right thing." Sarah sighed.

"Thank you. I appreciate this; I know this had to be tough."

"Yeah, but I'll be okay." Sarah smiled, still unsure if she made the right choice.

"Okay baby, you did the right thing. Now it's time to get on with your life. We're late." Chimed Sheree.

"Yes mama. Take care Carter," said Sarah

"You too."

"Carter?"

"Yes, Ms. Sheree?"

"If Saint Elizabeth won't take you back, I'm always available." Sheree said, grinning like a Cheshire cat.

∎∎

By the time Sarah walked into rehearsal, Claire was livid. "How dare you prance in here an hour late," she yelled.

"I'm sorry Mr. La Salle; I had a very important errand to run…" Sarah tried to explain.

"And it couldn't wait?"

"Obviously not," interrupted Sheree. "Don't start today Claire, I'm warning you."

"The least you could do was call," Claire admonished.

"My phone died. Again, I apologize."

"Mr. and Mrs. Mouton have been gracious enough to let us use their family chapel. Show some gratitude." Claire said rolling her eyes.

"Everybody, calm down. She's here now." Cate interrupted. "Are you ready for your big day sha'?" She continued turning her attention to Sarah.

"Yes, Mrs. Mouton. And thank you so much for allowing us to use your chapel. I will be forever grateful." Sarah said giving her a hug.

The little chapel was the only place where slaves were allowed to marry. Nathan Mouton had bought it from an old plantation that was going to tear it down, and restored it for his wedding to Cate. It's where their son's married their wives, and where all of their children and grandchildren were christened. Ethan was practically raised oh the estate with Reid and Elizabeth, so they were honored to allow him to marry there as well, regardless of the circumstances.

"Sha', you are family now, call me Gran." Cate said squeezing Sarah's hand.

....

Knowing Elizabeth and Sarah's history, Carter was hesitant to meet Sarah when she called. She told him she just wanted to help him make amends with Elizabeth, but Carter was not prepared for the information that he received.

Turns out that there were more pictures than originally published. The Blog was given specific instructions to print the story and pictures as they did. Sarah had gotten her hands on a couple of pictures that showed the man's face clear as day. Although Carter knew in his gut that he was set up, he was speechless when he realized that Ethan was the culprit.

"Should've known it was him," Colby said after Carter explained everything.

"Why do you say that?"

"He bowed out too easily." Colby pointed out.

"I mean okay, I figured that at some point before the wedding he would try to change Elizabeth's mind. But this kind of betrayal? It's one thing to throw salt on me, but he smeared Elizabeth's reputation in the process. What kind of love is that?" Carter asked

"I have no clue. I guess he got desperate. Enough about him. Now that you have the truth, what are you going to do with it?" Colby asked.

"I have no clue." Carter sighed.

TWENTY-ONE

Elizabeth sat on the side of the tub with her feet in the water. She opted to stay and help the mothers with wedding preparations instead of going out. She was beyond tired. The chapel was beautiful, the ladies really outdid themselves. She knew Ethan and Sarah would really be surprised tomorrow.

"May I come in?" she heard her grandmother ask after a quick knock on the door.

"Sure Gran. What are you still doing up?" Elizabeth asked glancing at the clock.

"I was going over a few details with Eloise for tomorrow when Reid called my office." Cate explained.

"What's wrong, is he okay?" Elizabeth asked concerned.

"Yes, sha'. Although he wasn't calling for himself."

"Gran. Can you please tell Reid to tell Ethan that it's over? With or without Carter, there is no me and him." Elizabeth sighed.

"Well that's good to know, because he wasn't calling for Ethan." Cate laughed.

"Well what did he want?"

"He wanted to know if it was okay for Carter to come over." Cate explained.

"You're kidding, right?"

"Not at all."

"Has Reid lost his mind?"

"Nah, he's just concerned for your well-being."

"Well, you said no. Didn't you?"

"Lizzie, Carter loves you."

"I'm not so sure about that Gran." Elizabeth said softly.

"Well, I am. I told you, Gran knows these things."

"Okay Gran, can you just tell Carter I'll call him tomorrow."

"Tell him yourself."

"What?"

"Carter is here." Cate laughed.

"Where?" Elizabeth asked in shock.

"You kids need to talk." Cate said.

"So, let me get this straight. Carter is here, in the house. And you're about to let him come in my room?" Elizabeth asked skeptically.

"He needs to be gone before your grandfather wakes up in the morning. If he catches Carter in here, Gran don't know nothing." Cate warned with a chuckle.

"Bring him in," Elizabeth sighed with defeat.

A few moments later Cate returned with Carter, "talk." She said closing the door behind her.

Elizabeth looked Carter up and down, savoring every moment. Every time she saw him he took her breath away, and tonight was no exception. He was wearing a white Gucci dress shirt, black Gucci jeans, and black Gucci loafers. The man looked good enough to eat, she thought to herself.

"I've missed you," it was Carter that spoke first.

"What do you miss Carter?"

"I miss starting and ending my day with you. I miss your sweet texts, and your silly selfies. I miss seeing you smile, and hearing your laugh. I miss your scent on my pillow and your hair in my face as we sleep. I just miss you."

"Wow," Elizabeth said trying to maintain her composure. Carter was not going to make this easy.

"Baby, do you remember how easy it used to be?" he asked softly

"When?"

"Every day, until you put your wall up. I mean you did try to fight it. But still, it was easy. Then the minute that you realized that you cared about me, shit changed. And we've been doing this crazy back and forth ever since."

"Things are just so complicated Carter." Elizabeth sighed.

"How? We are crazy about each other. You were ready to give us a real shot until those stupid pictures popped up."

"And I asked you not to make me regret it."

"You did. But come on Elizabeth, do you really think that's me?"

"I'm not really sure Carter."

"Yes you are Elizabeth."

"Okay, maybe it's not you." She conceded.

"Okay, we're getting somewhere."

"Hold your horses Carter. Seeing that picture reminded me of what's at stake. And it's more than I have to give."

"More than you have to give, or more than you want to give."

"Both."

"Damn, woman. What do I have to do to show you that I'm yours? One hundred percent completely yours. Please just tell me, anything. I'll do it." Carter pleaded.

Elizabeth was not prepared for this. She was sure that he would walk away. Just like Ethan and Mason had in the past. Neither of them fought for her, maybe Carter was different after all. "I don't know Carter."

"Baby, you are almost as stubborn as you are beautiful." He sighed.

"Look Carter, I have a long day tomorrow and I really need some rest. I promise I'll call you in the morning." Elizabeth said heading back to her bathroom and closing the door behind her.

"If you say so," Carter said watching her walk away.

• •

Elizabeth lay back in the tub replaying her conversation with Carter. She decided that she would sleep on it, and whatever she felt the minute she woke up is what she would do. She closed her eyes feeling a slight sense of relief.

Carter watched the bathroom door intently. He couldn't just let her go. He'd come too far. "Here goes nothing," he said to himself.

"Knock, knock" Carter said, softly tapping on the door.

Elizabeth eyes flew open. Carter was still standing on the other side of the door. "Come in."

"You sure?"

"Yeah,"

"I just wanted to let you know that I'm leaving and that I love you." He said trying to keep his gaze on Elizabeth's face.

"Give me a minute, I'm just going to wash my back, then I'm getting out."

"Do you want some help?"

"Sure," Elizabeth smiled, handing Carter the loofa.

Carter slowly washed Elizabeth's back and butt. He tried counting to one hundred, and then he tried saying his ABC's. He was trying anything to ignore the yearning he felt. When he couldn't take it anymore he turned Elizabeth around and gave her a deep kiss. He felt her body soften against his. Carter dropped to his knees and pulled Elizabeth to his waiting tongue. First he kissed the top of her mound, and then he started to slowly kiss and suck her clit.

"Carter," Elizabeth moaned.

"Yes, baby."

"I love you," Elizabeth moaned.

That was all he needed to hear. Carter stood up and kissed Elizabeth long and full on the mouth. He lifted Elizabeth from the tub, and carried her to the bed. He laid her down and removed his shirt. He stopped for a moment to admire the perfect beauty of the woman he loved. He dropped to his knees again and began to kiss Elizabeth tenderly on her inner thighs.

"Baby," she moaned again.

Carter spread her legs and stuck his tongue deep inside of her pussy. He missed the taste of her. Carter relentlessly kissed and sucked Elizabeth to the brink. Just as he thought that he would explode, he felt Elizabeth's juices flood his mouth.

Carter stood up and pulled off his jeans. He lay on top of Elizabeth and kissed her tenderly. "I love you Elizabeth." He said as he entered her.

Elizabeth's squeal let him know that she had missed him too.

"You okay baby?" he asked.

She shook her head yes, with tears glistening in her eyes.

Carter started his stroke slow, and intense, gradually increasing his pace. He decided that being inside of Elizabeth must be what heaven felt like.

"What are you trying to do to me?" Elizabeth moaned as she came.

"Do you want me to stop?" Carter smiled.

"No," she sighed. Pulling Carter into a kiss.

Elizabeth and Carter made love in silence, their bodies moving to their own rhythm. Elizabeth knew that there was no going back. She wanted Carter, and she was tired of playing games. She opened her eyes just as she was about to cum. "I love you," she said again, as she felt her body explode.

"I love you back," Carter said, as they came in unison.

TWENTY-TWO

"Good shit," Reid said peeking his head inside of Elizabeth's room.

Elizabeth jumped "you scared me Reid." She said. She frantically searched her room for Carter. Thinking maybe last night was a dream.

"He's on the floor," Reid said. Smiling at the relief on her face. "Y'all made up?"

"Yeah," Elizabeth blushed. "Thank you."

"It was nothing. But y'all need to get it together before the Calgary gets here." Reid said closing the door behind him.

• •

"Wake up, sleepy head." Elizabeth said planting a kiss on Carter's cheek.

"Good morning, beautiful." Carter smiled.

"When did you get on the floor?"

"Around five, I didn't want your grandfather to catch me in bed with you. So I got dressed and lay on the floor, hoping to minimize the damage."

"That was sweet of you," Elizabeth blushed.

"Anything for you baby," Carter smiled.

"Are you going to stay for the wedding? Or do you need to get back to Charlotte?"

"What do you want me to do?"

"I'd like t if you can stay. But if you can't I understand."

"Then I'll stay."

"Good. I'll tell my nanny to make sure that you're at the table with Taj and Ashton. Reid's date will probably sit with you guys as well."

Carter looked puzzled, "Why would Reid bring a date?"

"Cause Reid always has a date," Elizabeth laughed, rolling her eyes.

"What's this?" Elizabeth asked picking something up off of the floor.

"Shit," Carter said taking it out of her hand.

"Not again, Carter. Damn." Elizabeth exclaimed.

"No, baby. It's not like that." Carter tried to explain.

"Well what is it like?" Elizabeth asked, snatching it back. She turned it over and gasped. "What the fuck is this Carter?" She asked staring at him in disbelief.

The hurt in her eyes told Carter that he had fucked up again.

"Why would you do this Carter?" Elizabeth asked.

"Do what?"

"So had I not believed you, you were going to pretend like it was EJ?" she yelled.

"Of course not Elizabeth. Listen to me." Carter tried to explain.

"What's the heck is going on? Take it down a notch, before someone hears you." Reid said closing the door behind him.

Elizabeth simply handed the picture to Reid.

Reid looked at the picture unbothered and handed it to Carter, "You didn't tell her?"

"I didn't want to cause any more confusion," he explained.

"Will one of you tell me what the fuck is going on?" Elizabeth yelled.

"Dang, B! You are loud as shit!" Jenna said joining the commotion.

"What are you doing here?" Elizabeth asked surprised to see Jenna.

"I decided to come early," Jenna explained.

"Anyway," Elizabeth said giving Jenna the side-eye. "One of you start talking." She said turning her attention back to Carter and Reid.

"I hired a P.I. to do some digging. This is what he gave me. The pictures have been authenticated. Whoever sent them to The Blog, omitted the pictures that clearly showed Ethan's face." Carter explained, reciting the story that he'd made up. He didn't want to throw Sarah under the bus.

"Why didn't you tell me this last night?" Elizabeth asked.

"That was my intention. But I wanted you to just trust my word, to have faith in me. And like I said, I didn't want to create any more confusion."

"You have to be able to understand that B" Jenna said trying to help.

"Baby, listen. We got caught up, and I decided to wait."

"Are you sure it's not because you thought I'd go running back to Ethan?" Elizabeth asked.

"I actually thought the opposite." Carter laughed. "I know that Ethan needs you guys by his side today, that's all. I know that you and Ethan have history, but I also know in my heart that you love me."

Elizabeth softened, "No more secrets Carter."

"I can do that."

"Does EJ know that you guys have this picture?" Elizabeth asked.

"I told him about it after Carter and I talked, he seemed just as shocked as we were." Reid explained.

"Humph…" Said Elizabeth unconvinced.

"Well, I think he's lying." Jenna added her two cents.

"You know what. I don't even care. But eventually the truth will come to light." Elizabeth said.

"Now that that is settled," Carter began, "I need you to sneak me out of here Reid."

"Let's go." Reid laughed.

"Reid, will you call my nanny and tell her to make sure that Carter and your date are seated with Taj and Ashton?"

"I'll call her, but I'm not bringing a date." Reid explained.

"You? The bachelor of the year? You're not bringing a date?" Elizabeth laughed.

"Nope, this evening I'll be solo."

"Solo, but…" Carter looked puzzled.

"Come on man; let's get you out of here." Reid said shuffling Carter out of the room.

TWENTY-THREE

Sheree looked at her daughter with tears in her eyes. She'd almost pushed her daughter into her footsteps all those years ago. She was barely an adult when she plotted to get her thirteen-year-old daughter knocked up by a wealthy boy. She simply wanted a better life for her child; sometimes Sheree thought she had done Sarah more harm than good. She had never forgiven herself for Sarah losing the baby. That was all behind them now; her wildest dreams were about to come true.

"I love you baby," Sheree said.

"Love you too mama," Sarah smiled.

"I'm going to go check on Ethan, I'll be back."

■■■

Sheree stood at the door in disbelief. She didn't know if she should stop the scene in front of her or run the other way. She decided to leave the room unseen. As she hurried down the corridor, she ran smack into Carter. "Hey Carter," she said frazzled.

"Hey, Ms. Sheree, you okay?" Carter asked, concerned.

"I'm okay. Boy you look betta and betta er'time I see you." Sheree cackled.

"You look nice as well. Have you seen Elizabeth?" Carter asked.

"Uh yeah," she stammered. "Third door on the left." Sheree said scurrying away. She knew she was dead ass wrong, but oh well.

Carter counted the doors, and tapped slightly on the door before entering. What he saw stopped him dead in his tracks. He could feel his anger rise. This could not be happening. He stormed across the room and tore Ethan off of her. Then he saw it, the hummingbird tattoo.

"What the fuck are you doing, man?" Ethan yelled. Heather stood there wide-eyed.

"I was just about to ask you the same thing." Carter said with disgust.

"Why do you care, and what the hell are you doing here any damn way?" Ethan spat.

"I was invited by the maid of honor," said Carter.

"Sooo… this is the quarterback?" Heather smiled seductively licking her lips.

"Yeah, that's him." Ethan said rolling his eyes.

"Ethan, look. Elizabeth knows that it's not me in those pictures." Carter explained.

"Happy for you. Can you go now?" Ethan said impatiently.

"Why did you do this?" Carter asked.

"Look man, I'm just trying to get some pussy before I put on the old ball and chain." Ethan said exasperated.

"That's not what I'm referring to."

"Oh, the pictures?" Ethan laughed.

"Yeah, the pictures." Carter said shaking his head.

"You know why."

"No, really. I don't."

"Come on Carter. I know jocks aren't the smartest people in the world, but you can't possibly be that dumb." Ethan said with an evil grin.

"Whatever man," Ethan said walking out of the door disgusted; he decided that was his confirmation. He immediately felt sorry for Sarah.

"Damn," Ethan said kicking a chair after Carter left.

"Lemme ask you something," purred Heather.

"What now Heather?" asked Ethan.

"If Elizabeth walked in here right now and asked you to stop the wedding, would you?"

"Without hesitation," Ethan said.

"And what about me?" Heather asked sadly.

"What about you? You knew what it was from the jump."

"Please don't marry Sarah," Heather began to cry.

"Do you like your condo?" Ethan asked Heather.

"Yes."

"What about your Lexus? You like that too?"

"Yes."

"And how about those little blue boxes?"

"Baby, I love those."

"Thought so. Look we don't have time to fuck now and I need to bust this nut. So get on your knees, and suck my dick. Nothing's going to change after the wedding. You know the only reason I'm getting married is for my trust fund."

"You promise baby?" Heather purred.

"I promise, now suck daddy's dick."

■■■

"Hey sexyface," Elizabeth smiled at Carter.

"Wow, you look stunning. I think you get more beautiful every time I see you," he smiled in awe.

"Stop that," Elizabeth blushed. "I love you," she smiled giving Carter a quick kiss, marveling at how easily the words rolled off of her tongue.

"I love you back."

"I love you more," Elizabeth giggled.

"I loved you first," Carter said pulling Elizabeth into a deep kiss.

TWENTY-FOUR

Elizabeth smiled as Sarah made her way down the aisle. She could honestly say that she was looking forward to starting over and forging a friendship with her. Elizabeth looked over at Ethan and saw a tear roll down his cheek. He winked as Sarah reached the altar.

Just as everyone sat down, the doors of the church opened. In sauntered Heather. Sarah's mouth dropped. Claire looked like she'd seen a ghost. Amelia was on fire, and Sheree looked like she would vomit. Reid, Jenna and Elizabeth all stared in disbelief as Heather walked towards the front of the church. Elizabeth caught the quick gaze between Mathieu and Paul; it was not lost on them who she was. Amelia stood, and looked like she was going to tackle Heather, so she hurriedly took a seat on the third row.

"No this bitch didn't," Jenna said breaking the silence.

Ethan Senior shook his head. He seemed to be the only person that didn't realize who Heather was. Ethan stood there smiling like an idiot. In that moment, it was clear to Elizabeth that he was indeed the culprit behind the pictures.

"Seriously, Ethan!" shrieked Sarah in disbelief.

"Don't you dare cause a scene," Claire warned her.

Elizabeth looked at her Godmother in shock, "Nanny how could you."

"Not now Elizabeth," Claire said quickly.

Elizabeth looked from her mother to her father. She could tell they were both seething. But she knew neither of them would say anything publicly. Her father did not believe in public spectacles.

"If not now, then when?" Sarah yelled. "Ethan I know, that I have not been perfect, but this is just too much."

"What's too much?" he smirked.

"Your jump-off having the nerve to attend our wedding," Sarah cried.

"Get over yourself," Ethan whispered.

"Stop this nonsense right now EJ!" Ethan Senior admonished.

"Dad, I haven't done anything." Ethan laughed.

Sarah could not believe this was happening. And she couldn't believe that Ethan was behaving so cavalierly. She turned to Elizabeth, "I'm so so sorry Liz."

"Don't apologize, it's not your fault," Elizabeth said glaring at Ethan. "Are you okay Sarah?"

"I will be."

Elizabeth pulled Sarah into a tight hug. She had no idea why Ethan was behaving this way.

"Thank you," Sarah said Hugging Elizabeth back. Then she turned to Ethan, "I love you so much Ethan, but I really can't do this anymore." She said taking off her veil.

"Stop the dramatics Sarah," Ethan said rolling his eyes.

"Make that hussy leave, son." Ethan Senior fussed.

"It's okay, Mr. LaSalle. I'll go. Goodbye Ethan." Sarah said running from the altar.

Ethan stood there dumbfounded.

"Boy you better go after my baby if you know what's good for you," Sheree threatened.

"Nah, she'll be back," Ethan said smugly.

Whap. The sound of Sheree's hand landing on Ethan's cheek startled the crowd. Without another word, Sheree stormed out of the chapel, with a few of Sarah's friends and family trailing behind her.

"This is going to be the talk of New Orleans," Jenna whispered to Elizabeth.

"The show is over folks. There will be no wedding today," Ethan laughed loosening his tie.

"Maybe there will be."

"You cannot be serious," Ethan said turning on his heels.

"Aren't you tired of playing games babe? I know I am. I've tried to convince myself that this was just a fling, but I cannot deny any longer that I'm in love with you. I'm happiest when I'm with you. And when we aren't together, I'm counting down the seconds until I can see you again."

Elizabeth's mouth was wide open, as was much of the crowd. She was in shock.

"Babe, please. Don't just stand there. Say something. Say you'll marry me. Tell me you'll be my wife."

"Yes," Jenna said through tears. "Yes Reid, I'll marry you."

Filthy Little Rich Girl III

Copyright © 2015 by Beast Mode
Publications
ISBN: 0692438165
ISBN-13: 978-0692438169

www.ingramcontent.com/pod-product-compliance
Lightning Source LLC
Chambersburg PA
CBHW020410150626
46554CB00012B/592